Fireworks and Forever

Noel Jade

Fireworks and Forever

Publisher:

Independent Publisher

First Edition: December 2024

For more information about the author, e-mail yearroundnoel@yahoo.com

Contents

Chapter One

Sparks in the Snow

Ellie Harper

The first sign of trouble is the flicker.

I glance at the trailer's outdated ceiling light as it blinks once, twice, then dims to a murky orange. For a fleeting moment, it teeters on the edge of holding on. I lean back, holding my breath, willing the light to stay alive.

But then it sputters, flickering weakly, the yellowish glow trembling as if summoning one final burst of energy before surrendering. The bulb lets out a faint, high-pitched buzz, like the whine of a dying firefly, before going dark completely. Shadows deepen in the sudden absence of light, plunging the room into a dull, lifeless gray.

"No, no, no," I groan, my stomach knotting as the quiet settles in. I already know what's coming next.

As if on cue, the small space heater near the door coughs out one last valiant hum, its rattling fan slowing to a painful stop. For a brief moment, there's nothing but silence—heavy, unnatural, and far too loud.

Then comes the crackle, sharp and menacing, from the old outlet. The acrid scent of something burning hits my nose, and I freeze, staring at the heater, half-expecting it to burst into flames.

The trailer settles with a groan, as if mocking me for daring to believe this could've been a normal night. A thin puff of smoke curls upward from the socket, the acrid smell already filling the air. I barely have time to process it before a loud pop echoes beneath the floor, sharp and final, like a warning shot.

For a moment, everything hangs in uneasy silence.

And then it happens.

A bright shower of sparks bursts from the base of the trailer like fireworks gone horribly wrong, lighting up the snowy ground outside. From my tiny window, I catch sight of something even worse—one of the sparks lands on the elaborate strand of holiday lights draped across the nearby oak tree. The lights flicker frantically, then go completely dark.

"Oh, come on!" I shove open the door, the icy air biting at my face as I rush outside. My boots crunch against the snow, each step quick and heavy as I take in the full disaster.

The trailer sits under the pale moonlight, more pitiful than usual with a thin trail of smoke curling lazily from its undercarriage. The string of lights has gone completely dark, leaving a gaping void in what had been, just moments ago, a cheerful winter display.

The oak tree looks especially sorry now, its bare branches weighed down by the darkened strands of lights that had once been glowing proudly. Somewhere, Gloria is probably feeling a disturbance in the force.

A series of sharp, deliberate stomps echoes through the night, growing louder with each step. Someone is clearly not thrilled about this turn of events.

"Seriously?" a low voice growls from the shadows.

Here we go.

The beam of a flashlight slices through the darkness, and Liam Brookes steps into view, his imposing frame outlined against the faint glow of the snow-covered park. He towers over me in a dark coat that's dusted with frost, his heavy boots crunching against the icy ground with deliberate, no-nonsense steps.

The bitter wind seems to cling to him, settling in the hard set of his jaw and the furrow of his brow. A man who brings winter itself wherever he goes.

In one hand, he holds the flashlight, its steady glow highlighting the sharp angles of his scowl. In the other, he grips a battered mug, steam curling from its contents in the cold night air. The image might've been almost relaxed—if it weren't for the look on his face, a combination of disbelief and irritation that completely destroys any hint of calm.

"What the hell did you do?" he snaps, his voice cutting through the quiet like the crack of a frozen branch. His tone is as sharp and unyielding as the icy wind whipping through the park.

"I didn't do anything," I shoot back, already bristling. Okay, sure, this is partially my fault. But there's no need to act like I've declared war on Christmas.

Liam shines the flashlight at the base of my trailer, then at the blackened section of the snow where the sparks landed. Finally, he sweeps it toward the tree, where his once-perfect holiday display now looks... less perfect.

"Unbelievable," he mutters, shaking his head. "You couldn't have waited until after the holidays to blow something up?"

"I'm sorry," I say quickly, because I know I need to get ahead of this. "Something must've shorted out. The wiring in the trailer is ancient, and—"

"Yeah, no kidding," he interrupts, glaring at me.

I bite back a sarcastic comment, reminding myself that this is not the time to pick a fight with my grumpy neighbor. Not when I already have enough on my plate.

He crouches near the base of the trailer, inspecting the damage like a crime scene detective piecing together evidence. His brow furrows deeper, and the light from his flashlight catches on the edge of the damaged socket.

"This isn't just old wiring," he mutters. "This is a safety hazard waiting to happen."

I cross my arms, the cold seeping through my sleeves. "Thanks for the diagnosis, Doc. I'll be sure to consult you for my next disaster."

He shoots me a look, the kind that could curdle milk. "You're lucky this didn't start a full-on fire."

"Well, you're lucky I didn't electrocute myself, so I guess we're even," I snap.

His lips twitch—whether in annoyance or amusement, I can't tell—but he doesn't respond.

"I'll fix it," I offer, though I have absolutely no idea how.

Liam raises an eyebrow, his expression a mix of incredulity and faint amusement. "You're going to fix my lights?"

"Well..." I trail off, gesturing helplessly toward the darkened display. "Maybe not personally. But I can—uh—contribute? Pay for new ones or something?"

Liam exhales sharply, shaking his head like he can't believe he's having this conversation. "Forget it. Just... try not to burn the whole place down while you're at it."

"Wow," I mutter under my breath, shifting my weight from one foot to the other. "Merry Christmas to you, too."

"What was that?" His sharp tone makes me snap my head up.

"Nothing!" I chirp, all faux innocence.

His eyes narrow, and for a moment, I think he's going to press the issue. Instead, he crouches to inspect the damage to my trailer, muttering something about safety hazards and fire codes under his breath.

Great. Exactly what I need—a lecture from the Trailer Park Grinch.

As Liam pokes around, clearly unimpressed with the state of my wiring, I try to focus on the positives. At least I wasn't hurt. At least I'm not completely stranded. And at least I won't have to deal with this much longer.

That last thought should be comforting, but it settles awkwardly in my chest, like a puzzle piece forced into the wrong space.

I let my gaze drift toward the horizon, where the dark shapes of the mountains loom like silent sentinels. Somewhere out there is my future—a tiny apartment in the city, a job that doesn't involve power outages or campy holiday decorations, and a life that finally feels like my own.

A life where I don't have to answer to grumpy neighbors or half-broken heaters or questions about why I'm still here. A life that's shiny and new and filled with endless possibilities.

But as I stare at the snow-dusted peaks, their edges sharp against the star-streaked sky, the vision feels oddly flat. Like a postcard from a place I'm not sure I want to visit anymore.

This place has been fine for a pit stop, but it's not where I'm meant to stay. Maple Creek is too small, too predictable, and entirely too comfortable for someone like me.

Right?

I've spent my whole life dreaming about more. Chasing it, even when it felt like running on a treadmill, going nowhere. But here I am, stuck in a trailer park with smoke curling from its undercarriage and a man who could probably win a gold medal in scowling.

"Ellie," Liam's voice snaps me back to the present, breaking through the cold night air.

"Yeah?"

"You're going to need help with this," he says, straightening up. He gestures toward the trailer, his tone flat but unmistakably annoyed.

I cross my arms, the chill in the air sinking deeper into my skin. "What kind of help?"

"The kind that involves not setting your wiring on fire again," he replies, brushing snow off his gloves with brisk, annoyed motions. His breath hangs in the air between us, sharp and visible in the cold. "Look, I'll take a closer look tomorrow, but you're going to owe me for this. Big time."

"Fine," I say, though the words stick in my throat like unripe fruit. The weight of the moment presses against my chest, and I cross my arms tighter. I hate being indebted to anyone—especially him.

It's not just the idea of owing Liam something that bothers me. It's the way he said it, like he already knows I'll mess this up again, like helping me is a burden he's grudgingly willing to shoulder because no one else will.

And maybe that's the worst part. He's probably right.

Liam doesn't wait for thanks. He casts me one last exasperated look, his jaw tight as he mutters something under his breath.

The crunch of his boots against the snow echoes as he turns and heads back toward his trailer, his shoulders stiff against the cold night air. "Incompetent," I catch him grumbling as he disappears into the shadows.

I stand there for a long moment, the wind biting at my face and my pulse still thrumming with the tension he left behind.

I can't decide what annoys me more—his attitude or the fact that he's not entirely wrong.

My wiring is a mess. My trailer is an accident waiting to happen. And, unfortunately, Liam Brookes is probably the only person around here with the know-how to fix it.

Still, I can't help but bristle at the way he looked at me, like I'm some helpless disaster waiting to be cleaned up.

"Well, joke's on you, buddy," I mutter to myself, kicking at a patch of snow. "I've got a plan."

It's simple enough: stick it out for the next two weeks, get this trailer patched up enough to survive the trip, and leave Maple Creek behind for good.

As I glance back at the darkened tree, the smoke still faintly curling from my trailer, and the sad, scorched remnants of what used to be holiday cheer, the plan feels more fragile than ever.

The image of Liam walking away, his shoulders stiff against the cold, lingers in my mind. The way he muttered under his breath, like helping me was a foregone conclusion, like he's already resigned himself to stepping in when things inevitably fall apart again.

I should be mad. Furious, even.

Instead, I feel something else—something I don't want to name. It's not gratitude, not exactly. More like the quiet realization that I don't hate it when he's around, even when he's bossy and impossible and entirely too good at fixing things.

Okay, maybe the plan isn't perfect.

But it's all I've got.

For now.

Chapter Two

Deals and Distractions

Liam Brookes

It starts with a knock.

No, more like a pounding.

I pause mid-sip of my coffee, glancing at the clock on the wall. Seven a.m. Too early for this nonsense.

The pounding comes again, louder this time, followed by Gloria Thompson's unmistakable voice. "Liam, I *know* you're in there!"

Of course, it's Gloria. Who else would show up at this hour with all the urgency of a SWAT team raid? With a sigh, I set down my mug and open the door.

Gloria beams at me like she's just been crowned queen of Maple Creek Trailer Park. She's wearing a bright red coat with fur trim, and her curls are tucked under a Santa hat that's seen better days.

"Merry Christmas Eve Eve!" she declares, as if that's a thing people actually say.

I squint at her. "What do you want, Gloria?"

"Help," she says brightly. "Obviously."

I brace myself, but it's not enough to prepare me for what comes next.

"We need Ellie Harper on the planning committee for the potluck," she says. "And since you're already helping her with the trailer, you can make sure she doesn't wiggle out of it."

"I'm not on the planning committee," I remind her.

"Yes, but you're handy. You fix things." She waves a mittened hand as if that explains everything. "And this potluck needs fixing, Liam. It's our chance to make a real impression on Councilman Greene before he votes on the developers' proposal."

I groan. There it is—that dreaded word: developers.

Everyone in the park has been on edge since the proposal came through last month. Some big-shot real estate firm wants to tear down Maple Creek Trailer Park and turn it into "luxury townhomes." The vote isn't until after the new year, but Gloria's convinced the potluck could be the key to swaying Greene's decision.

"Can't you rope someone else into this?" I ask.

"Ellie's perfect for it," Gloria says, undeterred. "She's creative. She's got energy. And honestly, we need some fresh ideas. No offense to Doris, but her mashed potato bar isn't going to blow anyone's mind."

"It's a potluck," I point out. "Not a Michelin-star restaurant."

Gloria ignores me, craning her neck to peer past me into the trailer. "Where's Lila? She'll back me up on this."

"Still asleep," I say quickly, blocking her view. Gloria loves my kid, but she's not above recruiting her for one of her schemes.

"Well, think it over," she says, patting my arm. "But don't take too long. Time is ticking!"

With that, she bustles off, leaving me to nurse my coffee and my growing headache.

* * *

By the time I finish fixing Ellie's trailer later that afternoon, Gloria's words are still rattling around in my head.

Ellie stands a few feet away, her arms crossed against the cold as she watches me work. Her trailer looks slightly less pitiful now that I've patched up the wiring and cleaned up the scorch marks.

"Well?" she asks when I finally straighten up.

"It's safe," I say grudgingly. "For now. But you'll need to replace most of this wiring if you want it to last."

Her shoulders slump a little, though she somehow still manages to plaster on a polite, "Thanks."

"You're welcome," I mutter, the words leaving my mouth like they've been dragged out against their will. Being polite to Ellie Harper—Miss Sunshine-and-Sketchbooks—isn't exactly my default setting.

She tilts her head, her bright eyes narrowing suspiciously. "What's the catch?"

"What do you mean?" I ask, feigning innocence even though I can feel her gaze drilling into me.

"You're being... nice," she says, her tone laced with an almost theatrical disbelief, like I've just committed a crime against nature. "That usually comes with strings attached."

I hesitate, because she's not wrong.

Ellie crosses her arms, raising an eyebrow. "There it is. That pause. That's your tell. Come on, out with it. What's the catch?"

"Fine," I admit, rolling my eyes as I lean back against the doorframe. "There is one thing."

Her expression shifts instantly to mock horror, one hand flying to her chest as if I've just revealed I'm about to sell her trailer to the highest bidder. "I knew it!"

"Relax," I deadpan, crossing my arms. "I'm not asking for your firstborn or whatever dramatic thing you're imagining."

"Good," she shoots back. "Because Lila already has dibs on my hypothetical firstborn for babysitting practice."

"Lucky kid," I reply dryly. "But no. All I want is for you to stop trying to set the park on fire."

She glares at me, though the corners of her mouth twitch like she's fighting back a smile. "It wasn't on fire."

"Close enough," I shoot back, gesturing vaguely toward the offending outlet. "And by the way, your wiring is basically a death trap. You're lucky I'm nice enough to deal with it."

"Nice," she echoes, her voice dripping with sarcasm. "Right. That's totally the word I'd use to describe you."

"Careful," I say, leaning in slightly, lowering my voice just enough to make her shift. "You're dangerously close to ungrateful."

Ellie lets out an exaggerated huff, throwing her hands up. "Fine! Thank you, Liam. Thank you so much for saving my disaster of a trailer. Is that better?"

I smirk. "It's a start."

She narrows her eyes again but doesn't argue, and for a moment, it's just the two of us standing there, the cold biting at our skin and the faint hum of the park in the background.

Finally, she shakes her head, muttering something under her breath that sounds suspiciously like, "Grumpiest knight in shining armor ever."

I catch it, but I don't respond. Mostly because she's not wrong.

"I need you to help Gloria with the potluck," I say, crossing my arms. "She's roped me into it, and now I'm roping you in, too."

Ellie groans, throwing her head back in dramatic protest. "I can't!"

"You can," I counter. "And you will. Unless you want to pay me for all this work." I gesture to the trailer for emphasis.

Her mouth opens, then closes again. She knows she's got no choice.

"Fine," she says at last, her voice dripping with reluctance. "But I'm not happy about it."

"Join the club," I reply.

* * *

That evening, I end up back where the action is, surrounded by the usual chaos. Ed and Doris are in the middle of a spirited debate over potluck etiquette.

"It's a potluck, Ed," Doris says, exasperation thick in her voice. "No one cares if your casserole dish matches the serving spoon."

"Presentation matters," Ed argues, adjusting his glasses with the air of someone defending their doctoral thesis. "Councilman Greene's going to notice if we half-ass this."

"Councilman Greene isn't coming for the casserole dishes," Doris retorts, crossing her arms. "He's coming because Gloria wouldn't stop calling his office."

I lean against the wall, watching the exchange with mild amusement. This kind of back-and-forth is standard around here, part of the trailer park's weird charm.

"Dad!"

I look up to see Lila racing toward me, her curly hair bouncing as she waves something in the air.

"Careful!" I warn as she skids to a stop in front of me, nearly losing her balance.

"Look!" she says, holding up a flyer that looks suspiciously like one of Gloria's creations—bold fonts, glitter accents, and a completely unnecessary clipart image of a turkey.

"What is this?" I ask, taking it from her.

"It's the list!" Lila says excitedly. "Gloria said Councilman Greene is bringing people with him. Like, important people."

I scan the flyer, and sure enough, there's a bold headline that reads: *"Welcome Councilman Greene and Guests!"* Below it is a short list of names that I don't recognize—developers, real estate investors, a few city council members.

"Guests," I mutter, frowning. "Great."

"They're here because of the zoning stuff," Lila says, like it's obvious.

I glance down at her. "What zoning stuff?"

Lila rolls her eyes, like I've missed some critical piece of trailer park news. "Gloria says the council is deciding if the park stays a park or if it gets... what's the word?" She scrunches her nose, thinking. "Redeveloped."

My stomach tightens.

"Redeveloped?" I echo, my voice sharper than I intend.

"That's what she said," Lila replies, entirely unfazed by my reaction. "Like, turning it into apartments or something. She said this potluck is our chance to show the council why the park matters. So they'll keep it the way it is."

The flyer crinkles under my tightening grip, the paper soft and fragile against my palm as my thoughts churn.

* * *

Later, I corner Gloria near the dessert table, where she's fussing over a tray of cookies shaped like fireworks.

"Why didn't you tell me about this?" I demand, holding up the flyer.

She glances at it and shrugs, her expression unbothered. "I assumed you knew."

"Knew what? That the council is considering tearing this place down?"

"They're *considering* it," Gloria says, emphasizing the word like it makes everything better. "It's not a done deal."

"Gloria."

She sighs, lowering the tray of cookies and leveling me with a look. "Listen, Liam. This park isn't exactly prime real estate, but it's valuable. Developers have been eyeing it for years. The council has a vote coming up, and if we don't convince them that Maple Creek is worth preserving, well..."

Her voice trails off, but the implication is clear.

I glance around the room, taking in the mismatched decorations, the casserole dishes lined up on the tables, the neighbors laughing and chatting like nothing's wrong.

"This place is our home," I say quietly.

"I know," Gloria says, her voice softening. "That's why we need to show them what makes it special. If Greene and his friends see how much this park means to us, maybe—just maybe—we can stop them from turning it into a parking lot."

The stakes settle heavily on my shoulders as I step outside, the cold air biting at my face.

This park isn't perfect. The trailers are old, the roads are uneven, and the rent isn't always paid on time. But it's home.

And I'm not going to let anyone take that away.

From the corner of my eye, I see Ellie leaving her trailer, her sketchpad tucked under her arm. She catches sight of me and hesitates, her expression unreadable.

For a moment, I think about telling her what's happening—about the developers, the council, the fragile future of this park. But then I stop myself.

Because if she knows, it'll only give her another reason to leave.

And right now, I need her to stay.

* * *

Christmas Eve arrives with the kind of chill that seeps into your bones, the sky already streaked with soft shades of purple and gray as evening settles over Maple Creek.

Lila bursts into the kitchen as I'm pouring coffee, her energy unmatched despite the long day we've already had. She's wearing a red sweater with a snowman on it, complete with tiny bells that jingle whenever she moves.

"Dad! Come on, you're gonna miss it!"

"Miss what?" I ask, pretending to be more interested in the mug warming my hands.

She groans, throwing her head back dramatically. "The Christmas stuff! Everyone's bringing decorations to the hall, and Gloria said I could help set up the dessert table!"

"Lucky you," I say dryly, but I set the mug down and grab my jacket.

The hall is already bustling by the time we get there. The warm glow of string lights spills through the windows, and faint strains of Christmas music drift into the chilly evening air. Inside, familiar voices rise over the chatter, including a spirited debate about cranberry sauce: canned versus homemade. Across the room, Gloria moves with the determination of a woman orchestrating a grand performance, pointing people toward tasks like an air traffic controller.

"Dad, look!"

Lila's voice pulls me from the chaos as she races over, holding something in her hands. Her grin is so wide it threatens to split her face, her cheeks still pink from the cold.

"Look what Ellie gave me!" she says, holding up a little snow globe.

Inside, glitter swirls around a miniature trailer park scene—a snow-dusted trailer with a tiny wreath on the door, a few evergreen trees, and a picnic table with just the faintest touch of sparkling snow.

I blink, leaning closer to get a better look.

"Where'd she get that?" I ask, frowning slightly.

"She made it!" Lila announces proudly. "She said it's for the New Year's potluck decorations, but she let me pick one early. Isn't it pretty?"

I glance across the room, where Ellie stands near the makeshift stage, talking to Gloria. She's holding her sketchpad, flipping through pages as Gloria gestures animatedly.

"Yeah," I say slowly, my gaze lingering on Ellie. "It's pretty."

Lila hugs the snow globe to her chest like it's the most precious thing in the world, then darts off to show it to Ed and Doris. I watch her go, my thoughts heavier than they should be.

Ellie Harper is full of surprises.

* * *

A while later, as I untangle a string of lights for the hall's entrance, Ellie wanders over, her sketchpad tucked under her arm.

"Hey," she says, her voice casual but warm. "How's it going over here?"

"Could be better," I reply, holding up the tangled mess of lights.

She smirks, setting her sketchpad on the nearest table. "Need some help, or are you just planning to glare at that tangle of lights until it magically untangles itself?"

"Funny," I deadpan, though I hand her the offending strand of lights. "Knock yourself out, Picasso."

"Picasso was a painter," she says, arching a brow as she starts working on the knot with nimble fingers. "But sure, let's go with that."

The sound of the heater humming in the background mixes with the chatter of the hall as we work side by side. Her fingers move quickly, untangling what I thought was a lost cause, while I busy myself hanging the freed sections.

"So," I say after a moment, glancing at her. "The snow globe. Lila said you made it."

Ellie straightens slightly, her cheeks turning pink as she brushes a strand of hair from her face. "Oh, yeah. It's just something I've been working on. I thought it'd be nice for the New Year's decorations, you know, to give the place a little... charm."

"A little?" I scoff lightly, holding up another untangled strand of lights. "You made a whole miniature version of this park. That's more than a little charm."

She laughs softly, the sound light and musical as her hands pause mid-motion. "I guess I just wanted it to feel special. Like it's more than just another trailer park."

"It already is," I mutter, then clear my throat when her head whips toward me, her eyes widening slightly. "I mean, you don't have to go overboard with the glitter and glue for people to see that."

Ellie grins, her expression teasing now. "Is that your way of saying you like it?"

I shake my head, but a smirk pulls at my lips. "It's my way of saying I tolerate it. Barely."

"Tolerate it, huh?" She leans in slightly, her voice dropping to a mock-conspiratorial tone. "Lila told me you wouldn't stop staring at it when she showed you."

"I was trying to figure out how you crammed so much glitter into such a small space," I retort, but the warmth in her gaze throws me off balance.

"Well," she says with a shrug, returning her focus to the lights, "glitter makes everything better."

"Except cleanup," I grumble, shaking a particularly stubborn strand loose.

"Some things are worth the mess," she replies, her voice soft but pointed.

Our eyes meet briefly, and something unspoken passes between us before she looks away, her hands resuming their work.

"Yeah," I say quietly, more to myself than to her. "Maybe they are." Her eyes returning to mine catch me off guard, and I study her for a second. "You're good at that."

"At what?"

"Making things special."

Her eyes flick up to meet mine, and for a moment, something unspoken passes between us.

But then Gloria calls her name from across the room, and the moment breaks.

Ellie picks up her sketchpad, her movements a little hurried. "Guess I better get back to work."

"Yeah," I say, watching as she walks away.

The snow globe comes to mind again, its tiny, perfect world swirling with glitter and care.

And for the first time, I wonder if maybe, just maybe, she sees this place the way I do.

But then I push the thought away. People like Ellie don't stay in Maple Creek.

And I'm not about to make the mistake of hoping otherwise.

Chapter Three

Plans on Paper

Ellie Harper

I don't officially agree to anything.

Not at first, anyway.

When Gloria smiles at me like I've just volunteered to take over the world, I plaster on a half-hearted grin and nod in a way that says, *Sure, maybe, but probably not.*

But apparently, "sure" is enough for her.

"Wonderful!" she beams, clapping her hands like I've just solved world hunger. "We're going to make this the best potluck Maple Creek has ever seen!"

And just like that, I'm on the committee. Or team. Or whatever they call it when a handful of trailer park residents decide to throw a party.

I tell myself it's temporary, a small price to pay for Liam fixing my trailer. A means to an end.

Still, the thought of spending two weeks planning this thing—and inevitably bumping into Liam every other minute—does not fill me with holiday cheer.

"Welcome to the team," Gloria announces, thrusting a hefty binder into my hands with all the ceremony of someone bestowing the

Holy Grail. The binder, faded red with a slightly warped cover, proclaims *Potluck Plans: The Definitive Guide* in glittery cursive.

I open it cautiously, expecting to find blank pages or perhaps a token grocery list, but no—this thing is *packed*. Page after page of tightly packed handwriting and diagrams meet my eyes. There are lists for dishes, table assignments, and theme suggestions, each one color-coded and cross-referenced. One page features a timeline for the night of the event, complete with bullet points and hourly check-ins.

"Wow," I manage, flipping to a section labeled *Dessert Display Concepts: The Non-Negotiables.* "This is... thorough."

Gloria beams, clearly taking my stunned reaction as a compliment. "You'll get the hang of it," she says briskly, patting my arm in encouragement. "We'll meet tomorrow to go over your ideas. Be prepared to pitch something dazzling!"

Before I can protest, she winks and hurries off, her jangling Santa earrings disappearing into the next flurry of activity.

I'm left holding what might as well be a brick of paperwork and responsibilities.

I look down at the binder, its glittery title catching the light, mocking me. *Potluck Plans: The Definitive Guide.* It feels less like a guide and more like a trap.

This is why I don't get involved, I think as I turn to leave.

The community hall is still buzzing with activity as I make my way toward the door. Kids dart around with tinsel in their hands, chasing each other between tables. Ed and Doris are loudly debating the optimal number of marshmallows for sweet potato casserole—again. Gloria's voice rings out over the chaos, cheerfully commanding someone to "bring more twinkle lights, for heaven's sake!"

It's... a lot.

By the time I step outside, the cold air feels like a relief, sharp and bracing against my flushed cheeks. I clutch the binder to my chest as I walk back toward my trailer, the snow crunching softly under my boots.

The park is quiet now, the activity concentrated in the hall. Strings of lights dangle from trailers like mismatched necklaces, some blinking, some steady, some barely holding on. It's a haphazard charm I can't quite bring myself to dislike.

When I reach my trailer, I hesitate on the steps, the binder heavy in my arms. The last thing I want to do is dive into *Potluck Plans: The Definitive Guide,* but Gloria's voice echoes in my head, cheerfully urging me to "pitch something dazzling."

Inside, the heater hums faintly as I set the binder on the table and open it again. The pages stare back at me, unrelenting in their enthusiasm.

I flip to a section labeled *Table Themes: Where Creativity Meets Class,* skimming the bullet points. "Rustic Elegance," one heading reads, complete with subpoints about birchwood accents and seasonal florals. Another section boasts "Winter Wonderland," with an enthusiastic note in the margins: *Consider fake snow for dramatic effect!*

"Dramatic effect," I mutter, leaning back in my chair. "Sure, why not?"

For a moment, I think about closing the binder and forgetting this whole thing. But something stops me. Maybe it's the way Gloria's eyes lit up when she handed it to me, or the fact that Lila practically bounced out of her chair at the thought of decorating.

Or maybe it's the memory of Liam's quiet insistence that this park is worth fighting for.

I sigh, picking up a pen and tapping it against the table.

"All right, *Potluck Plans,*" I say, flipping back to the first page. "Let's see what you've got."

Hours later, I'm still at the table, surrounded by crumpled bits of paper and hastily scribbled sketches. My coffee mug sits abandoned, the contents long gone cold. The ideas are starting to take shape, albeit messily, but my exhaustion is starting to win out.

I glance toward the window, where the park is bathed in moonlight. It's quiet now, save for the occasional flicker of a Christmas light or the faint crunch of snow as someone walks by.

Maybe this potluck won't be a total disaster. Maybe.

As I gather up the scattered papers and close the binder, I realize something unexpected.

For the first time in a long time, I don't feel like running.

Not tonight.

* * *

The park has quieted now, the day slipping gently toward evening, but a different kind of life hums in the air.

Snow blankets the branches of the oak tree at the center of the park, softening its jagged silhouette into something almost delicate. Twinkling lights hang from trailers in every direction, each display unique—some strung with the precision of an artist, others haphazardly draped as though tossed up in a rush. There's no uniformity here, no HOA-approved symmetry. And yet, that's what makes it feel alive.

Ed and Doris' trailer, with its meticulously crafted wreath of plastic spoons painted in gold and silver, somehow manages to look both ridiculous and refined. I can practically hear Doris smugly defending their choice: "Recycling *and* creativity. Two birds, one stone."

Next door, Gloria's yard is chaos incarnate. Inflatable candy canes lean precariously to one side, as if caught mid-dance in the winter wind. The oversized Santa in her front yard deflates every few minutes, slumping over with a wheeze, only to rise again with stubborn determination. It's more slapstick than Santa, and I can't help but smile.

The air carries the faintest hint of woodsmoke, mingling with the sharper, nostalgic scent of cinnamon and cloves. Somewhere nearby, a neighbor's wind chimes jingle faintly, their soft, irregular notes threading through the stillness like whispers. My breath curls in small puffs before me, fading into the dusk as I walk past the trailers, each one a reflection of its owner's personality.

When I glance at my own trailer, I pause.

The patchwork repairs Liam made earlier catch the light from a nearby strand of blinking holiday lights. Mismatched aluminum and weathered siding are stitched together in a way that's undeniably practical but glaringly unpolished. It sticks out among the festive displays around it—a reminder of its imperfections and, if I'm honest, my own.

Still, there's something about it that tugs at me. Not pride, exactly, but something gentler. Gratitude, perhaps. The trailer's flaws are obvious, but it's standing. Functional. Home, for now.

And isn't that the truth for me, too? I'm not where I want to be—not yet. But I'm here. Still moving forward, even when it feels like I'm piecing myself together with duct tape and prayers.

I let out a slow breath, my gaze lingering on the mismatched panels.

When I was younger, before life taught me to tuck dreams away like fragile keepsakes, I wanted to start my own business. Nothing extravagant—just something that took the fleeting magic of a celebration and made it last. Weddings, birthdays, even quiet moments like this.

I used to scribble ideas into spiral-bound notebooks, names scrawled across the top of every page.

Fireworks and Forever.

That was the one I always came back to. It felt like a promise: capturing the ephemeral beauty of fireworks and grounding it in something that could stay. Something that could *belong.*

But then came bills and responsibilities, the way life sweeps you off your feet but never in the way you hope. Dreams fell to the back burner, replaced by "good enough" and "maybe later."

I shake my head, trying to push the thought away, but the ache of it follows me like a shadow as I turn toward the community hall.

The hall is alive with color and sound, though the hum is quieter now, more focused. Inside, a group of kids huddles over a pile of cardboard boxes, glitter, and glue, their chatter a mix of playful bickering and bursts of laughter.

Lila's curly hair bounces as she leans over her project, her lopsided pigtails sticking out like she's channeling pure chaos. "No, no, *like this!*" she insists, grabbing a tube of glitter glue with the authority of an artist defending her masterpiece.

Liam stands in the doorway, his arms crossed but his posture loose. His gaze doesn't waver from Lila, the kind of look that could melt a glacier—protective, steady, ready to spring into action if one of those glitter-coated boxes dares to pose a threat.

He doesn't see me standing just outside, watching him.

For a fleeting moment, I let myself imagine the life I once dreamed of. Not just a business, but something more. A community. A family. Fireworks painting the sky, laughter spilling out into the night, memories etched so deeply they last long after the colors fade.

I lean against the frame of my trailer door, the ache in my chest unfamiliar. It's not painful, not really. It's something softer—a longing I haven't let myself acknowledge for years.

And for the first time, the thought of staying doesn't feel impossible.

Liam shifts his weight, leaning into the doorframe as Lila glances up at him, beaming with pride. He smiles back, and the sight twists something in my chest, a mixture of joy and hesitation.

He doesn't notice me, and I don't call out to him. Instead, I push the trailer door open and slip inside.

Once the door shuts behind me, the outside world fades. But Liam's steady presence and Lila's joyful chatter stay with me, lingering like a spark that refuses to fade.

* * *

Later that evening, I spread the potluck binder across the tiny table in my kitchenette. The red cover wobbles slightly, refusing to lie flat after years of use, and I weigh it down with the edge of a ceramic mug. Beside it, I lay out a blank sketchpad and a tin of colored pencils I found buried in the back of my closet earlier today.

I'm not sure why I kept them. Most of my old art supplies were donated or tossed years ago, back when the idea of sketching felt like a waste of time. I haven't drawn anything since high school, when I used to fill sketchbooks with dreams too big for Maple Creek—ideas for store windows with cascading flowers or elaborate stage sets full of lights and texture.

But now, as I stare at the blank page and the mess of notes in the binder, something stirs. My fingers hover over the pencils, itching to begin, but there's a hesitation I can't quite shake.

The overhead light hums faintly, casting a yellowish glow that softens the sharp edges of the cramped space. Outside, the wind presses against the trailer's thin walls, a low, constant whisper that seems to nudge me forward.

Finally, I pick up a pencil, the familiar weight settling into my grip like an old friend.

The ideas come slowly at first, tentative and unpolished: centerpieces made from mason jars and tea lights, tablecloths patterned with snowflakes, a photo booth with a winter wonderland backdrop. I sketch loose shapes and details, the lines uneven but full of potential.

The snow globe centerpiece idea from earlier finds its way onto the page again, this time with more precision. I add tiny trailers inside the globes, each one unique—one with a wreath on the door, another with tiny candy canes propped against its steps. The more I draw, the clearer the scene becomes, like the pieces of a puzzle snapping into place.

Outside, the occasional burst of laughter from a nearby trailer filters in, mingling with the faint crackle of my old heater. I glance up, my gaze drifting to the frost-covered window. For a moment, I let myself imagine the scene coming to life—the soft glow of the mason jar centerpieces, the sparkle of glitter snow globes catching the light, the photo booth overflowing with props and laughter.

The thing is, I like this part: the planning, the imagining. It's the doing that always trips me up. The part where people expect you to show up, to stick around and see things through.

My stomach twists at the thought, but I push it aside, focusing instead on the sketch in front of me.

The world outside fades as I lose myself in the process. The colored pencils glide across the page, layering soft blues for the snow and warm yellows for the glow of candlelight. I smudge the edges with my fingertips, giving the drawings a softness I always loved when I was younger.

I don't notice the time slipping by until my hand cramps, forcing me to set the pencil down. I lean back in the chair, stretching my fingers as I glance at the clock.

It's past midnight. I should probably get some sleep, especially with Gloria's meeting tomorrow.

But instead, I pick up another pencil.

Because for now, this feels good.

Even if it's temporary.

Even if I don't stay.

I sketch long into the night, filling page after page with ideas. There's a freedom in it that I hadn't realized I missed, a sense of creation that doesn't care whether the ideas ever make it past the paper.

By the time I finally set the sketchpad aside, the first hints of dawn are brushing the edges of the sky outside. I gather up the papers, stacking them neatly on the table, and glance down at the final drawing I'd finished—a snow globe, not just with trailers but with tiny people in the scene.

One figure is sitting on the steps of a trailer, gazing at a jar of fireworks wishes.

It's a ridiculous, overly sentimental touch, but something about it makes me pause.

Because I know that scene, don't I?

It's here, in this place I keep telling myself isn't home.

The heater clicks off with a final hum, and the chill of the early morning seeps in. I shiver slightly but don't move right away, letting the weight of that realization settle over me like the blanket I'm too tired to grab.

I might not stay.

But tonight, I let myself imagine that I could.

Chapter Four

Glitter and Grumbles

Liam Brookes

Ellie Harper has opinions.

Strong ones, apparently.

"That's a terrible idea," she says, her voice cutting through the cold like a whip.

We're standing in the middle of the community hall, surrounded by a half-assembled collection of tables, chairs, and mismatched decorations. The place smells like pine and cinnamon, thanks to Doris' insistence on "setting the mood" with potpourri.

Ellie crosses her arms, glaring at the folded piece of paper in my hand like it's personally offended her.

"It's efficient," I counter, holding up the table layout I sketched last night.

"It's boring," she shoots back.

I take a deep breath, counting to three before responding. "It's a potluck, Ellie. Not a royal wedding."

Her eyes narrow. "That doesn't mean it has to look like a cafeteria."

I glance at the tables, already draped in plain white tablecloths. "What's wrong with simple?"

"Simple is fine," Ellie says, snatching the paper from my hand with a flourish and jabbing her finger at a particularly dull section. "This, however, is not fine. This is bland."

My jaw tightens as I cross my arms. "It's not bland. It's minimalistic."

"It's boring," she counters, her voice so cheerful it almost hides the insult. Almost. "There's a difference between clean and coma-inducing, Liam."

I open my mouth to argue, because there's nothing wrong with a straightforward, no-frills approach. But before I can get a word in, Lila bursts into the room, carrying a container of glitter so large it might as well be classified as a weapon.

"Ellie!" she chirps, practically skipping over to her new favorite person. "I brought the sparkles!"

Ellie's face lights up like Christmas morning. "Oh, perfect! You're a lifesaver, Lila."

"Or an accomplice," I mutter, eyeing the glitter like it's about to stage a hostile takeover.

Ellie ignores me entirely, taking the container from Lila and shaking it slightly, her expression turning thoughtful. "Hmm. I'm thinking we add some to the centerpieces and maybe the banners..."

"Add?" I cut in, raising a skeptical brow. "You can't add glitter to everything. This isn't a preschool art project."

Ellie tilts her head, her smile dangerously sweet. "Why not? Afraid of a little sparkle, Mr. Minimalist?"

"Afraid isn't the word I'd use," I say flatly, leaning against the table. "Glitter doesn't stay where it's supposed to. It's chaos in a bottle."

"Chaos," she repeats, her grin widening as she opens the container with a dramatic flourish. "Exactly. A little chaos is what this place needs."

"Lila," I say, turning to my daughter, who is already bouncing on her toes in excitement. "Do not—"

Too late.

Lila reaches into the container with both hands, grabbing a fistful of glitter and flinging it into the air like she's summoning magic.

"Lila!" I groan as a cascade of tiny, sparkling particles rains down on the table, the floor, and—of course—me.

Ellie's laughter rings out, bright and unapologetic. "Look at that, Liam! Chaos."

I glare at her, brushing glitter off my sweater to no avail. "You know what they say about glitter, right? This stuff never goes away."

Lila giggles, delighted with herself, while Ellie smirks, clearly enjoying my misery.

"Oh, come on," Ellie says, her voice laced with amusement. "Don't be such a grinch. Look how happy she is."

I glance at Lila, who's currently twirling in a circle, leaving a trail of glitter on the floor. She's beaming, her cheeks flushed with excitement, and for a moment, I can't bring myself to be too mad.

Still, I level a look at Ellie. "You're a bad influence."

She gasps, placing a hand over her chest in mock offense. "Me? A bad influence? I'm just bringing a little sparkle into your life, Liam."

"More like a mess," I mutter, though the corner of my mouth twitches despite myself.

Ellie leans in slightly, her voice low and teasing. "You could use a little mess in your life."

For a second, I forget to argue back, caught off guard by the way she says it—with just enough warmth to make it sound like a challenge.

As much as I hate to admit it, she's good at this. In the span of a few minutes, she transforms the table from a bland, functional surface into something that actually looks... inviting. The plain white tablecloth doesn't look so dull anymore, not with the addition of a gold runner and a few strategically placed candles.

"See?" she says, stepping back to admire her work. "Not boring. And no one's fallen asleep yet."

I glance around the room, noticing for the first time how everyone seems to gravitate toward her. Doris, who's usually quick to critique anyone's decorating decisions, nods approvingly at the centerpiece Ellie just finished. Even Ed, who's supposed to be working on the lights, pauses to offer a rare compliment before shuffling back to his ladder.

It's not just the decorations, though. It's Ellie.

She has this way of drawing people in, of making the chaos seem less like a problem and more like part of the fun.

I shake my head, trying to push the thought away. "You've got glitter in your hair," I say instead.

She reaches up, her fingers brushing through her curls. "Do I?"

"A lot of it," I say, smirking slightly. "You look like you lost a fight with a Christmas ornament."

Ellie sticks her tongue out at me, but there's no real venom behind it. "Better than looking like a grumpy lumberjack."

"Grumpy lumberjack?" I repeat, raising an eyebrow.

She grins, leaning against the table like she owns the room. "Yeah. You've got the whole rugged thing going on, but you frown so much it's practically a trademark. If you smiled more, you might scare fewer people away."

"I'll keep that in mind," I mutter, though the corner of my mouth twitches despite my best efforts to suppress it.

Before I can come up with a retort, Lila dives for another fistful of glitter. In one swift motion, she flings it into the air, sending another wave of sparkly chaos cascading over the table—and me.

"Ellie," I groan, glaring at her as Lila erupts into giggles. "Control your accomplice."

Ellie crosses her arms, pretending to consider it for all of two seconds. "Hmm, nope. She's her own woman. I can't hold her back."

"I'm begging you," I say flatly, brushing at my sweater, which now glitters like I've been attacked by a rogue disco ball. "This isn't funny."

"It's a little funny," she counters, her grin widening.

"Ellie," I warn, though there's no real heat behind it. She's too busy laughing to notice.

"Relax," she says, grabbing a towel from the supply bin. "It's festive. You could use a little sparkle in your life, Liam."

"It's a mess," I correct, watching as she steps closer with the towel in hand. "And it's everywhere."

"Here, let me help," she says, already closing the distance between us.

"Ellie, I don't need—"

Too late. She starts patting my sweater with the towel, her movements deliberate but somehow softer than I expect. The fabric drags against the glitter, scattering some of it but not doing much to dislodge the stubborn particles clinging to me like a second skin.

"This isn't working," she mutters, her brow furrowing in frustration. Without hesitation, she tosses the towel aside and uses her hands instead, brushing at my chest with careful, deliberate motions.

Her touch is light, almost hesitant, and for a moment, I forget to protest. The warmth of her hands seeps through the fabric of my sweater, and I'm acutely aware of how close she's standing. Too close.

Her fingers linger longer than necessary, trailing over the glitter-streaked material like she's trying to fix more than just the mess. My chest tightens, the air between us feeling suddenly charged in a way I don't know how to navigate.

I clear my throat, stepping back abruptly. "That's enough," I say, my voice rougher than I intended.

Ellie freezes, her hands hovering mid-air, her cheeks flushing a soft pink. Her eyes dart up to meet mine, wide and startled, like she's just realized what she's done.

For a moment, neither of us moves. The noise of the room fades into the background, leaving only the sound of my heartbeat pounding in my ears. Her expression shifts—nervous, maybe, but there's something else there too. Something I can't quite name.

"Dad, you're sparkly!" Lila announces, her voice breaking the tension like a needle popping a balloon.

Ellie exhales sharply, her lips twitching into a relieved smile. Then she laughs—bright and unguarded, the sound spilling into the room like sunlight breaking through a storm cloud.

Despite myself, I feel the edges of my frustration soften. Lila's giggle is infectious, and Ellie's laugh has a way of worming its way into the cracks I've worked so hard to keep sealed. It's infuriating, how easily she can disarm me without even trying.

I glance down at my sweater, which still glitters obnoxiously under the dim lighting of the hall. "Glad you're both amused," I grumble, though my voice lacks its usual bite.

"Oh, come on," Ellie says, her smile turning teasing. "Admit it, Liam. Deep down, you're having fun."

"Fun," I repeat, deadpan. "Standing here covered in glitter because you and my daughter can't be trusted with craft supplies. Sure, Ellie. A blast."

She laughs again, a softer sound this time, and shakes her head. "You're such a grump."

"And you're impossible," I counter, though there's no real venom in the words.

Ellie tilts her head, studying me with a look that's too knowing for my comfort. "You know, I think you secretly like it," she says, her voice quiet but laced with amusement.

"Like what?" I ask, raising an eyebrow.

"The chaos," she says, gesturing around the room. "The glitter, the decorating, the back-and-forth. You act all annoyed, but I think you'd miss it if it weren't here."

Her words hit closer to the truth than I want to admit, and for a moment, I don't know how to respond. She's not wrong. As much as her relentless energy drives me crazy, it also does something else—something I'm not ready to put into words.

"Don't flatter yourself," I say finally, my tone gruff as I brush more glitter off my sleeve. "I'd be perfectly fine without the glitter."

But even as I say it, I know it's a lie. Because Ellie's right. The glitter, the laughter, the chaos—it's all part of her. And whether I like it or not, it's starting to feel like something I don't want to lose.

* * *

By the time the room is (mostly) decorated, the community hall has started to fill with the usual Christmas Day crowd.

Ed and Doris are locked in their usual debate, this time over the proper way to hang a garland above the dessert table. Their bickering is softened by the way they keep sneaking glances at each other, a silent language of affection running beneath the surface. The garland droops at one end, but it somehow adds to the charm.

The scent of roasted turkey and baked pies wafts through the air, mingling with the faint notes of *Jingle Bells* playing on the ancient sound system that crackles every few minutes. Plates clatter and voices rise in overlapping conversations, the chaos as comforting as it is familiar.

"You know it's not about the garland, right?" Doris says, adjusting the ribbon for the third—or is it fourth?—time.

Ed frowns at the uneven loop she's just tied. "What do you mean?"

"It's about showing we care," she says, stepping back to examine her work. "If this place looks thrown together, Greene and his cronies will say it's 'proof' we don't deserve to stay."

Ed pauses, the usual lightheartedness in his bickering fading as he considers her words. "You really think they'd tear this place down? After all these years?"

Doris presses her lips into a thin line, her eyes flicking to the kids at the dessert table, now attempting to outdo each other by stacking gingerbread cookies into precarious towers. "I think developers see numbers, not people. And if this councilman can't see what makes this place special, they'll pave over our memories without a second thought."

Her voice trembles slightly at the end, though she covers it by tugging sharply at the garland.

Ed leans in, brushing her hand aside so he can adjust the garland himself. "They'd have to fight me first." His voice is low, steady—strong in a way that makes Doris glance at him, her expression softening.

The weight of their words settles in the air, lingering even as they quietly return to decorating.

Across the room, Gloria is directing traffic near the entryway, her slightly askew Santa hat bobbing as she carries a stack of mismatched ornaments for the final touches. Behind her, the younger kids are wrangling the tinsel, each trying to claim credit for the most dazzling strand.

"They'll think it's dazzling, all right," Gloria mutters under her breath as she passes me, the ornaments precariously balanced in her arms. "If Greene's heart doesn't melt when he sees this place, he doesn't have one."

Ellie stands off to the side, her arms crossed loosely as her gaze sweeps over the bustling hall. There's something in her expression I can't quite pin down—like she's caught between amusement and disbelief, unsure whether to join the chaos or run from it.

Her eyes flicker to the kids wrestling with tinsel near the dessert table, to Ed now lecturing Doris about the "proper" pie-to-cake ratio, and finally to Gloria, who's barking orders like a drill sergeant in a Santa hat.

"What's on your mind?" I ask, stepping beside her.

She startles slightly, but her lips tug into a soft smile. "Just... it's a lot. Everyone's working so hard to make this special."

"Not just special," I correct, nodding toward Ed, who's now wielding a ladle like a gavel. "Important. They're trying to show Greene this place is worth fighting for."

Her brows knit together. "And what happens if Greene doesn't agree? You think he's going to be swayed by Doris' pie ratios?"

I snort. "If anyone can win him over with dessert math, it's Doris."

Ellie huffs a laugh, but it fades quickly. "Do you really think it'll work, though? The potluck, the decorations, all of this?"

I shrug, the weight of the question settling on my shoulders. "I hope so. But if it doesn't..." I trail off, not wanting to say the words.

She doesn't press me, but her gaze shifts back to the room, her lips pressing into a faint line. The kids are laughing, the lights twinkle overhead, and for a moment, even Ed and Doris' bickering feels like something worth preserving.

"You're quiet," I say, tilting my head toward her. "What happened to the woman who had ten sarcastic comments ready at all times?"

She glances at me, rolling her eyes. "Don't get used to it. I'm just... taking it all in."

Her tone is softer than usual, almost wistful, and for once, I resist the urge to tease her about it.

I follow her gaze, seeing the park through her eyes. The laughter, the quirks, the way everyone fits here, no matter how mismatched they seem.

"This place has its moments," I admit, grudgingly.

Ellie smiles faintly, but her eyes linger on Doris and Ed as they step back to admire their work. Their bickering has stopped now, replaced by a quiet conversation. I can't make out the words, but the way Doris rests a hand on Ed's arm tells me enough.

"What makes this place special?" Ellie asks suddenly, her voice low.

I hesitate, caught off guard by the question. "What do you mean?"

She tilts her head toward Doris and Ed. "What's the story here?"

I glance at the older couple, their heads bent close together as they fuss over the garland one last time. "Ed and Doris have been here longer than anyone else. He used to work as a welder, and she taught second grade before she retired. They raised their kids here."

Ellie's brow furrows slightly, her attention fixed on them. "And they never wanted to leave?"

I shake my head. "Nope. Doris says the city feels too big, and Ed can't imagine living in a place without a workshop. To them, this park is more than just home—it's where their lives happened."

Ellie's expression softens, her arms uncrossing as she tucks her hands into her pockets. "It must be hard, knowing it could all be taken away."

Her words hang in the air, and I can tell she's not just talking about the park anymore. She's thinking about what it means to have a home—something I'm not sure she's ever really let herself want.

"It is," I say finally. "But that's why we fight for it."

She doesn't respond right away, her gaze distant as if she's turning the words over in her mind. When she finally looks back at me, there's something new in her expression.

"I guess some things are worth fighting for," she says softly.

And for the first time since she got here, I think she might actually believe it.

Chapter Five

Midnight Confessions

Ellie Harper

The clock on the wall ticks past midnight, each movement a steady reminder that I should be in bed, not drowning in crumpled sketches and the mess of half-finished decorations scattered across the table. The faint smell of pine from the stack of garlands in the corner only adds to the sense that we're trapped in some kind of festive purgatory.

"I don't know how I let Gloria rope me into this," I mutter, erasing yet another jagged line on my hopeless drawing.

Liam, sitting across from me with his arms crossed like he's guarding a vault, raises an eyebrow. "Welcome to the club."

I glance at him, the exhaustion tugging at my lips twisting into something like a smirk. "You mean she doesn't just target me?"

"Oh no," he says dryly, leaning forward with a slow shake of his head. "Gloria's an equal-opportunity menace. She once convinced Ed to build an entire gazebo for a potluck. In February. I'm pretty sure his fingers almost fell off."

I can't help it—I laugh, loud enough that it echoes through the empty hall. "A gazebo? In February?"

"She called it a 'community centerpiece.'" Liam's voice drips with sarcasm. "You can still see it leaning sideways by the playground. Real centerpiece material."

"Well," I say, reaching for my pencil, "at least I only have to deal with paper and glitter. Count me lucky."

"You say that now," he replies, his tone grim. "Wait until she gets you into her 'decorating ideas' phase. She'll have you balancing on a ladder in the snow trying to tie lights to a fifty-year-old tree branch."

"Sounds like you're speaking from experience."

He shrugs, but the corner of his mouth twitches, betraying the faintest hint of amusement. "Once. Never again."

"And yet, you're still here," I point out, arching an eyebrow. "Letting her boss you around."

Liam shifts in his chair, leaning back like he's settling in for a long argument. "Gloria's... persistent. And she means well. Besides, someone's got to step up when she gets these wild ideas."

"Oh, so you're her knight in shining armor?" I tease, tapping my pencil against the table. "How noble of you."

He snorts, the sound low and unimpressed. "More like her mule. She says jump, and I just hope I don't break an ankle."

"Wow. Such enthusiasm. I'm inspired."

"Glad to be of service," he deadpans.

I shake my head, still smiling as I add a flourish to the corner of my sketch. "Seriously, why do you do it? Why not just say no?"

There's a pause, just long enough for his brow to furrow slightly. "Someone has to. If it's not me, it'll be Ed. And he's already got his hands full trying to keep Doris from redecorating their trailer in neon pink flamingos."

The corners of my mouth twitch. "A selfless hero, indeed."

Liam gives me a look—half amused, half exasperated—and shakes his head. "Call it what you want. But Gloria usually has a point. Eventually."

"Eventually?"

"After a lot of yelling and poorly timed Christmas carols, yeah."

I laugh again, the sound less out of amusement and more out of sheer disbelief at how ridiculous this all is. It's easy, being like this with Liam. Easier than I thought it would be, considering how much he seems to grumble at everything I say.

For a moment, the pencil in my hand hovers above the page as I glance at him. There's something steady in the way he leans back in his chair, a quiet responsibility that lingers behind his dry remarks.

"So," he says, breaking the silence, "what's the grand vision for this potluck, anyway? Besides glitter and chaos."

I roll my eyes, holding up my sketch. "This. Tables arranged like an actual event, decorations that don't scream 'last-minute garage sale,' and maybe—just maybe—convincing people like Greene that this place is more than just a patch of land."

Liam studies the sketch for a moment, his head tilting slightly. "You've got talent," he says finally.

The compliment catches me off guard, and I blink at him. "Uh, thanks?"

He shrugs, like it's no big deal. "I mean it. You've got an eye for this kind of thing."

"Careful," I say, narrowing my eyes playfully. "Say too many nice things, and I might start thinking you like me."

"Let's not get carried away," he shoots back, but there's a warmth in his voice that wasn't there before.

I look at the sketch again, suddenly feeling a little less hopeless about the whole thing. "What about you?" I ask. "What's your vision for the potluck?"

"Survive it," he says immediately.

"Wow. A visionary."

"I aim high," he says with a smirk.

The easy rhythm between us surprises me. I didn't expect this when I first met Liam—the surly, frowning guy who seemed to think sarcasm was a second language. But sitting here, sharing jokes in the middle of a half-decorated community hall, I realize there's more to him than the grumpiness.

There's steadiness. Dependability. A quiet humor that sneaks up on you if you let it.

And I think I like it.

I push the thought aside, focusing on my sketch again. But I can feel his gaze on me, the weight of it somehow both grounding and unsettling.

"You're not bad at this, you know," he says after a moment.

"At what? Doodling?"

"At giving a damn," he says simply.

The words land heavier than I expect, and I glance at him, unsure of how to respond. He doesn't say anything else, just leans back in his chair and crosses his arms like he hasn't just cracked me open with a single sentence.

The clock ticks on, the smell of pine hanging in the air. And for the first time, the thought of spending the next few days working alongside Liam doesn't feel so daunting.

Maybe—just maybe—it might even be nice.

* * *

We fall into a rhythm after that, working side by side in comfortable silence.

Liam cuts lengths of ribbon with the kind of precision that makes me suspect he's better at this than he lets on, while I sketch out centerpiece designs, my pencils scattering across the table in a chaotic rainbow.

"You're good at that too, though," he says suddenly, nodding toward my sketchpad.

I pause, caught off guard. "At what?"

"Drawing. Planning. Making things look… nice."

I shrug, trying to downplay the compliment. "It's just doodling."

"It's more than that," he insists, his tone softer now. "You've got an eye for it."

The sincerity in his voice throws me, and I look away, focusing on the paper in front of me. The lines blur slightly as I try to absorb what he said without letting it sink in too deep.

"I used to want to do this kind of thing," I admit quietly, shading the edge of a snowflake. "Design. Decorate. Create stuff that makes people happy."

"What happened?"

The question hangs in the air, not heavy or probing, just… there. I could brush it off, move past it like I usually do when people ask about my past. But there's something about Liam—steady, patient—that makes me want to answer.

"Life happened," I say finally, the words coming out more bitter than I intended. "Dreams don't pay bills. And in a place like this, they don't get you very far."

Liam doesn't argue or try to offer hollow reassurances. He just nods, like he gets it.

"My family was always moving," I say, surprising myself with how much I'm sharing. "My parents, my grandparents—we never stayed in one place for long. Trailer parks, rented rooms, the occasional couch when things got tight."

I glance down at my hands, tracing the edge of the sketchpad in front of me. The pencil feels small and fragile between my fingers. "They worked hard, did what they could to get by, but it was always temporary. Nothing ever stuck. And the idea of staying som ewhere... of settling? It felt like giving up. Like admitting we didn't have a way out."

Liam's quiet for a moment, the only sound in the room the faint rustle of ribbon as he sets it down.

"And you don't want to end up like them," he says, his voice low and thoughtful.

I swallow hard, nodding. "I can't. I don't know what stability looks like, but I know I can't live the way they did. I want something more. Something... different."

The words feel raw, vulnerable, and they hang in the air like an exposed nerve. But Liam doesn't look at me with pity or judgment. His gaze softens, like he's weighing what I've said, turning it over in his mind.

"City life isn't all it's cracked up to be," he says after a while, his voice low.

I glance at him, surprised by the shift in tone. "You sound like you know from experience."

He chuckles bitterly. "Yeah. I do."

He leans forward, resting his elbows on the table, his gaze distant. "My ex-wife loved the city. She wanted the hustle, the excitement, the endless possibilities. I wanted something simpler. Something steady. We tried to make it work, but... we wanted different things."

I wait for him to continue, sensing there's more to the story.

"She left," he says finally, his jaw tightening. "Took the dreams she had and moved on. I stayed here, where I knew I could give Lila the kind of life I wanted for her."

The honesty in his voice pulls at something in me. It's the most I've ever heard him say about his past, and I want to say something to fill the space, to offer some kind of comfort. But the words won't come.

Instead, I just nod, hoping he can see that I understand.

His eyes meet mine, and for a moment, the weight of his gaze makes me feel... seen. Like he gets it in a way most people don't.

Before either of us can say more, Gloria's voice breaks the quiet, startling us both.

"Oh good, you're still here!" she says, sweeping into the room with a clipboard in hand.

Liam groans, dragging a hand down his face. "It's midnight, Gloria. What do you want?"

"An update," she says briskly, as if she's running a Fortune 500 company instead of a trailer park potluck. "Also, I have news. Big news."

She sets the clipboard down with a dramatic flourish.

"The developers are sending someone to the potluck," she announces. "Apparently, they want to see what this place is all about before the council vote."

Liam's expression darkens. "You're kidding."

"Do I look like I'm kidding?" Gloria huffs. "This is our chance, Liam. If we can show them what makes this park special, maybe—just maybe—they'll reconsider."

I glance at Liam, expecting him to argue, but he doesn't. He just presses a hand to his temple, looking as tired as I feel.

"This place is special," Gloria continues, her voice softening. "You know that as well as I do. But we have to prove it to them. And that starts with this potluck."

Her words settle over us like a challenge, and for the first time, I feel a flicker of something I don't want to name.

Investment.

I shake it off, reminding myself that this isn't my problem. This isn't my home.

But when Gloria leaves and Liam turns back to me, his eyes heavy with unspoken worry, I can't help but feel it again.

Maybe it's not my home.

But right now, it feels like it could be.

* * *

Later, after Liam's gone and the sketches are packed away, I sit alone in my trailer, staring at the snow globe I made for Lila.

The faint light from the lamp on the counter bathes the room in a soft, golden glow, casting long shadows that stretch and shift with the occasional creak of the heater. Outside, the world is silent, muffled by the thick blanket of snow that's been falling steadily since nightfall.

In my hands, the snow globe feels lighter than it should, almost delicate. Inside, glitter swirls around a miniature trailer, cozy and bright, its tiny windows painted to glow as though there's a fire crackling inside.

I tell myself it's just a decoration. Something I made to pass the time, a little project for Lila. But deep down, I know it's more than that.

I turn the globe over, watching as the glitter settles at the bottom before another flick of my wrist sends it spinning again. It's mesmerizing in a way I didn't expect—watching those tiny flecks of silver and gold drift and swirl like they have nowhere better to be.

The trailer inside looks nothing like my family's trailers ever did. Those were always battered and practical, with rust creeping up the sides and wheels that looked like they'd fall off if you blinked too hard.

This one is perfect.

It's warm, inviting, like the kind of place that could actually feel like home.

Home.

The word feels heavier tonight, pressing against my chest in a way I can't ignore.

I've spent so much of my life running from the idea of home. Of settling. Of putting down roots that could be pulled out without warning. It was easier to keep moving, to treat every stop like a temporary detour on the way to something bigger, something better.

But sitting here, staring at this tiny world I've built inside the globe, I can't stop the questions from creeping in.

What if this is better?

The thought startles me, and I set the globe down quickly, as though letting it go will also let the idea slip away. But it doesn't.

It lingers, settling into the cracks I didn't realize were there until now.

My gaze drifts to the window, where the snow has piled up high against the glass, creating a barrier between me and the world outside. The park is quiet, the trailers dark and still, but I can picture it so clearly—Lila laughing as she twirls with a sparkler, Gloria fussing over the pie table, Doris and Ed bickering like they've been married a hundred years.

It's messy. Loud. Imperfect.

And I'm starting to care about it.

The realization sends a jolt through me, and I stand abruptly, pacing the small length of the trailer.

Caring is dangerous. Caring means risking heartbreak. It means putting myself in a position where I can lose something—or someone—that matters.

And this place?

It's on the verge of being lost already.

If the council doesn't side with us, if Greene isn't swayed by all the decorations and casseroles and heartfelt speeches, this park could be gone by spring. Paved over. Forgotten.

I close my eyes, leaning against the counter as the weight of it all settles over me.

For weeks, I've told myself I don't have a stake in this. That Maple Creek is just another stop, another place I'll leave behind when the time comes.

But now, I'm not so sure.

Because the truth is, I don't want to leave.

I think about Liam's steady presence, the way his voice softened when he talked about staying here for Lila. The way his eyes met mine tonight, filled with a quiet understanding that felt like it reached deeper than I wanted to let him see.

I think about Lila, her laughter lighting up the community hall, her sparkler waving like it was the only thing that mattered in the world.

I think about Gloria, who fights for this park like it's part of her soul, and the neighbors who come together to bicker and bake and make this place more than the sum of its parts.

The snow globe catches my eye again, the glitter finally settling in a perfect halo around the tiny trailer.

I pick it up, turning it over in my hands once more. This time, I don't shake it. I just stare, letting the silence fill the space around me.

This isn't just a decoration.

It's a piece of me. A reflection of something I didn't realize I was missing until now.

And for the first time in years, I wonder if I've found what I've been searching for all along.

I set the globe back on the counter, my fingers lingering on the cool glass before I step away. The questions are still there, circling like the glitter inside, but I don't have the answers yet.

All I know is that I'm not ready to walk away. Not yet.

Maybe not ever.

Chapter Six

Wishes in the Jar

Liam Brookes

The fireworks jar is Lila's favorite tradition. She hasn't stopped talking about it all week, pestering Gloria to pull it out of storage early and practically staging a one-girl campaign to make sure everyone takes it as seriously as she does.

Now, as she drags Ellie toward the community hall where the jar sits on display, her excitement radiates off her in waves, bright and unstoppable.

"Come on, Ellie!" Lila calls over her shoulder, her voice cutting through the crisp winter air. Her gloved hand grips Ellie's, tugging her forward with relentless energy. "You're going to love this!"

Ellie laughs, her breath visible in the icy breeze, a puff of warmth against the cold. The sound rings out like bells, light and infectious. "I'm coming, I'm coming! I don't think I've ever seen anyone this excited about a jar before."

"It's not just a jar," Lila huffs, her tiny bell-adorned boots jingling indignantly as she stomps ahead. "It's *the* jar."

I trail behind them, letting the gap grow just enough to watch without feeling like I'm intruding. Ellie lets herself be pulled along easily, her steps light and unhurried, her smile unguarded. She leans into the moment in a way only Ellie seems capable of, like she's been waiting her whole life to be whisked into someone else's world.

Lila's gloves are oversized and flecked with glitter that catches the faint light from the hall's windows, but she doesn't seem to notice or care. Her grip on Ellie's hand is firm and confident, like she's leading her into something magical, and Ellie doesn't resist for a second.

It's been a long time since I've seen Lila this excited, her face lit up like a sparkler. And longer still since I've seen her connect with someone the way she's connected with Ellie.

When we reach the storage shed, Lila practically skips ahead, finally letting go of Ellie's hand to crouch beside the jar.

It's sitting on a table near the entrance, and while it's technically just an oversized mason jar, Lila's work has transformed it into something special. Tiny fireworks are painted on the glass in gold and silver, their jagged edges gleaming under the hall's soft lighting. Ribbons in every color imaginable are tied around the lid, the tails trailing down like streamers.

"This is it!" Lila announces proudly, unscrewing the lid with dramatic flair. "The fireworks wish jar. Everyone writes down their wish for the new year and puts it inside. Then, at midnight on New Year's, we read them after the fireworks."

Ellie crouches beside her, the hem of her coat brushing the ground as she tilts her head to get a better look at the jar. "That's adorable," she says, her voice warm and genuine. "Who came up with it?"

"Dad," Lila says with a grin. She looks over her shoulder at me, her eyes sparkling with pride. "A long time ago, right, Dad?"

I shrug, leaning against the doorframe. "Long enough that I don't remember."

Ellie glances up at me, one brow quirking in playful disbelief. "You don't remember? You, Mr. Practical, came up with something as whimsical as a fireworks wish jar?"

I cross my arms, my mouth tugging into a smirk. "Don't let the grumpiness fool you. I've got layers."

Ellie chuckles, her eyes sparkling. "Noted."

Lila, unfazed by our exchange, is fully immersed in explaining the jar's history. "Dad started it when I was little, so we could remember all the things we wanted for the new year. And Gloria made everyone join in because she said it would 'foster community spirit.'"

"That definitely sounds like Gloria," Ellie says, laughing softly.

Lila nods sagely, like she's delivering ancient wisdom. "But now, it's tradition. Everyone has to make a wish."

Ellie reaches out, brushing her fingers lightly against the jar, her fingertips trailing over the glass fireworks. "What kinds of wishes do people make?"

"All kinds!" Lila chirps, reaching into the jar to stir the folded papers already inside. "But you're not supposed to read them yet, so don't peek!"

Ellie raises her hands in mock surrender. "No peeking. Got it."

Satisfied, Lila digs through a pile of blank slips on the table and hands Ellie one, along with a pen. "Here! You have to write one, too."

Ellie hesitates, the playful light in her eyes dimming slightly. Her hand lingers over the paper, but she doesn't take it right away.

"What's the matter?" I ask, stepping closer.

Her hesitation isn't dramatic, but it's there—a flicker of something I can't quite name. She tilts her head, biting her lip, and for a moment, I think she might refuse outright. The pen hovers over the slip of paper in her hand, the edge of it trembling slightly between her fingers.

"It's just a wish," Lila says gently, her young voice carrying an unexpected weight of understanding. She leans against the table, her jingling boots now still as she looks up at Ellie with wide, earnest eyes. "You don't have to tell anyone what it is at midnight. It can be just for you."

Ellie smiles faintly at that, the tension easing from her shoulders. Her expression softens in a way that almost makes me forget the hesitation I just saw. "Okay, kiddo. You're right." She takes the slip of paper, her fingers brushing against the pen as she starts to write.

Her gaze dips, and her hair falls slightly forward, shielding her face from view. But even from where I'm standing, I can see the way her lips press together, the faint crease forming between her brows as she scribbles.

Halfway through, though, she frowns, her movements halting. She crumples the paper in her fist with a sharp, frustrated motion.

Ellie exhales, the sound somewhere between a sigh and a quiet laugh, and reaches for another slip. Her movements are slower this time, more deliberate.

"Second thoughts?" I ask, keeping my tone casual.

"No," she says too quickly, a defensive edge to the word that betrays her. She doesn't look up as she scribbles something else—shorter this time, her pen pressing harder against the page. Without pausing, she folds the paper neatly and drops it into the jar.

The sound of it landing is barely audible, but Ellie watches it fall as though she's committing the moment to memory.

I don't ask what she wished for, and she doesn't offer to tell me.

Lila, meanwhile, is busily scribbling on her own paper, her tongue sticking out slightly in concentration. The jingling of her boots resumes as she rocks back and forth, her energy bubbling even in stillness. When she's done, she holds her paper up like a trophy, waving it proudly before slipping it into the jar with a dramatic flourish.

Then she turns to Ellie, her grin full of mischief.

"I'll tell you mine if you tell me yours."

Ellie shakes her head, smiling, her tension melting like snow under sunlight. "Nice try."

"Okay, fine," Lila says dramatically, throwing her hands in the air with a theatrical sigh. "But I'm still going to tell you mine!"

Ellie leans closer, her curiosity piqued as she tilts her head. "All right, what's your big wish, kiddo?"

Lila beams, clutching the jar like it's the key to some great secret. Her cheeks are flushed pink from the cold, and the spark in her eyes rivals the painted fireworks on the jar. "I wished for Dad to find a girlfriend."

The words hang in the air like a firecracker that didn't quite go off.

"Lila," I groan, my voice low and warning as heat creeps up the back of my neck.

"What?" she says innocently, her grin unrepentant. "It's a good wish!"

Ellie's laughter bubbles up, light and unrestrained, her eyes darting between Lila and me. "Well, it's definitely... ambitious." Her gaze lingers on me, the faintest hint of teasing lighting up her face.

I run a hand through my hair, the motion more habit than anything else. The cold air nips at my exposed fingers, grounding me in the moment. "All right, Lila. That's enough. Time to head inside."

"But Dad—"

"No 'but Dad.' Inside. Now."

Lila huffs dramatically, drawing it out like a character in a soap opera, complete with exaggerated arm gestures. Still, she grabs her coat and heads toward the hall, the jingling of her boots punctuating her reluctant steps.

Before I can follow, she spins around, pointing an accusatory finger at me. "You haven't made your wish yet!"

"I'm getting to it," I say, grabbing a blank slip from the table.

Her gaze lingers on me, eyes narrowing like she's assessing whether I can be trusted to follow through. It's the same look she gives me when I tell her she can't have ice cream before dinner—equal parts suspicion and challenge.

Finally, she turns and disappears through the door, her laughter trailing behind her like the faint jingle of a bell.

As the hall door swings shut, Ellie turns to me, her expression unreadable but tinged with curiosity. "So, what's your wish going to be?"

"Who says I'm making one?" I counter, my tone light but deflective.

Ellie tilts her head, a sly smile creeping across her face. "You heard Lila. It's tradition. Even Mr. Practical can't mess with tradition, right?"

I roll my eyes, but there's no real annoyance behind it. "We'll see."

She crosses her arms, leaning her weight against the edge of the table as if settling in to watch. "Go on, then. I'll wait."

The challenge in her voice is soft, teasing, but it sticks with me all the same. I pick up the pen, twirling it between my fingers as I look at the blank slip in front of me.

The truth is, I already know what I'd write. It's been rattling around in my head for weeks, unspoken but persistent.

But writing it down? That feels different.

Ellie doesn't press me, her gaze steady but unintrusive. For the first time in what feels like forever, I don't feel the need to fill the silence.

The pen pauses above the paper.

And then I write.

I write quickly, folding the paper before she can get nosy.

Ellie's attention shifts just as I slip the paper into the jar. Her eyes narrow, and her lips twitch in amusement. "Are you going to tell us what it is?"

"Nope," I say, shaking my head, keeping my tone flat.

"Not even a hint?"

"Nope."

She crosses her arms, leaning against the table as her grin sharpens. "Come on, Liam. Is it 'World Peace' or something even more predictable like 'a new wrench set'?"

"Predictable?" I shoot her a look, raising an eyebrow. "You've known me five minutes, Harper. How would you know what's predictable?"

Her grin widens. "Oh, I've got you figured out. Big, strong, brooding guy who secretly writes 'No glitter' on his New Year's wish every year. How close am I?"

I snort, shaking my head. "You're not even in the same galaxy."

"Okay, fine. Maybe it's something mysterious and deep like, 'I wish my neighbors weren't a total pain.'" She taps her chin, pretending to think it over. "No, wait, that one's too obvious."

I glare at her, though it lacks any real heat. "You're lucky I don't charge you for this kind of attitude."

Her laugh is quick, a warm sound that bounces off the quiet of the room. She takes a step closer, propping herself on the edge of the table as she looks between me and the jar. "Seriously though, it's nice. You doing this every year. Lila really loves it."

I glance at the jar, shrugging. "It's just a tradition."

"Maybe," she says, her tone light but pointed. "But not all traditions are worth keeping. This one is."

Her words hit heavier than I expect, sneaking past my defenses. I glance at her, surprised by the sincerity in her voice. For a moment, the space between us feels smaller, the chill sneaking under the door pushed aside by something unspoken. I wonder if she realizes what she just said—or if she even knows what it means to someone like me.

Ellie tilts her head, her smile returning to its usual playful curve. "Fine, keep your secrets. But don't think this is over."

"Wouldn't dream of it," I mutter, shaking my head as she flashes me one last grin and heads toward the hall.

The door swings shut behind her with a quiet creak, leaving me alone with the jar. My fingers brush against its edge, the cool glass grounding me for a moment.

To find a family to dream with.

The words I scrawled earlier linger in my mind, fresh enough to sting. I didn't expect them to feel so loud now that I've written them down. I didn't expect Ellie—her teasing, her laughter—to make them echo louder.

Her laugh plays faintly in my memory, mingling with Lila's chatter. I think about the way Ellie teased me without malice, her tone not mocking but… light. Like she didn't expect me to be someone I'm not. Like it was okay just to spar with her, like equals. Her energy feels like a spark in the middle of this cold winter, breaking through the monotony I've convinced myself is fine.

I shake my head and let out a sharp breath. Focus.

This jar's tradition is about Lila. About giving her something to look forward to every year. That's all it is. It doesn't matter how Ellie fits into it. Or if I can already tell she's going to wedge herself into more corners of this place than she realizes.

It doesn't matter. Not at all.

Right?

But standing here, with Lila's wish still ringing in my ears, I can't push it down anymore.

Ellie isn't just passing through, not really. She's lighting things up, making this place—and maybe even me—feel different.

And the thought of her leaving makes my chest tighten.

The wish jar has always been simple. A way to mark time, to remind Lila that it's okay to dream even when things feel shaky. I started it when she was too young to understand why her mom wasn't around anymore. Back then, I didn't have the right words to make her feel safe, so I gave her a ritual instead. Something we could count on, year after year.

At first, it was just the two of us, scribbling our wishes onto scraps of paper that I cut from grocery bags. I'd write down things like "a healthy year" or "more sunny days," while Lila's wishes were always grander—ponies, castles, sparkly shoes that lit up when she walked.

But over time, the jar grew. Gloria caught wind of it, and suddenly, it wasn't just our little thing anymore. The whole park joined in, writing their own wishes, folding their dreams into tiny paper corners, and slipping them inside.

Now, it's a tradition for everyone. For Ed, who wishes for good fishing weather. For Doris, who pretends she doesn't believe in "this sentimental nonsense" but still sneaks in a wish every year. For the kids, who scribble wishes for new toys or endless snow days.

Somewhere along the way, the jar stopped being just a way to distract Lila and became something more—a reminder that even in a place like this, where life can be unpredictable and hard, it's okay to hope. To dream.

I run a hand over the lid, the worn glass cool beneath my fingers. The ribbons that Lila tied around the top last year are frayed now, their once-bright colors dulled. But they're still there, fluttering faintly in the draft from the door, a quiet testament to how much this jar has weathered alongside us.

Ellie's laughter from earlier replays in my mind, clear and full of light, and I realize something: she fits here. In a way I didn't see coming. Maybe the park needed someone like her—a force of nature who doesn't seem to notice the cracks in the walls or the peeling paint because she's too busy imagining what could be.

And maybe, just maybe, I needed her too.

My fingers brush against the jar one last time before I turn toward the hall, my boots crunching against the icy ground. The chill in the air doesn't bother me as much now. I slip inside, letting the warmth of the room envelop me, and find Ellie standing near the dessert table, chatting with Lila.

She's holding a plate of cookies, gesturing animatedly as she talks, her face lit up with an energy that feels impossible not to notice. Lila is hanging on every word, her laughter bright and free, and I feel that tightness in my chest again.

Wishes are just that: wishes.

But for the first time in years, I find myself hoping one might come true.

Chapter Seven

Dreams Unfolded

Ellie Harper

The community hall is quiet now, the faint hum of the heater the only sound as I fold up the last chair. The evening's laughter and chatter have faded into memory, leaving behind an empty space that feels too big, too still.

Lila ran off hours ago with a gaggle of kids, their giggles echoing into the cold night as they scattered to their homes. Liam ducked out not long after, muttering something about needing to check on his trailer. That left me alone to finish cleaning up.

I told Gloria I didn't mind. It's easier to work in the silence, to let my thoughts wander without anyone poking at them. Except now, with the last decorations boxed up and the chairs stacked against the wall, I find myself lingering.

The fireworks wish jar sits right where Lila left it, ribbons fluttering softly as a draft sneaks under the door. The paint on the jar catches the faint light, the hand-drawn fireworks shimmering like they still carry the promise of magic.

I shouldn't touch it. I don't mean to touch it. But as I pick it up to move it to the storage shelf, a folded slip of paper slips free and flutters to the table.

"Shoot," I mutter, setting the jar down carefully as I reach for the stray paper. My fingers brush the edge of the table, and my gaze drifts out the window. Beyond the glass, the park stretches out under the moonlight, a patchwork of trailers and snow-covered lawns.

It's easy to see why developers would want this place. The park sits on prime real estate—close to the highway and just a few miles from the new industrial center the town's been trying to expand for years. From a business perspective, it's a goldmine.

But standing here, surrounded by mismatched decorations and the faint scent of pine, it's impossible to see this place as anything but home. A place where kids grow up building forts out of cardboard boxes, where neighbors argue over cranberry sauce recipes but always show up when it counts.

I shake my head, brushing off the thought as I pick up the paper.

I don't intend to open it. But my fingers hesitate, and before I can stop myself, the fold loosens, revealing Liam's neat handwriting.

To find a family to dream with.

The words are simple, but they hit me harder than I expect.

A family to dream with.

Not flashy or ambitious, not the kind of wish I would have written when I was younger. Back then, my dreams were all about escape—of running so far and so fast that no one could catch me. But this wish... it's quieter, deeper. It tugs at something inside me I don't want to name.

I refold the paper carefully, slipping it back into the jar, but the words linger, echoing in my mind like the fading notes of a song I can't stop humming.

When I finally leave the hall, the cold bites at my skin, the kind of chill that settles into your bones. The snow crunches under my boots as I make my way back to my trailer, my breath puffing out in white clouds that vanish almost as quickly as they form.

The first thing I notice when I step inside is the cold. The heater's off again—of course—and the air is sharp enough to make me shiver. I try to shake it off as I rummage through the closet, pulling out the duffel bag I've had since high school.

I throw it on the bed and start packing, grabbing clothes and toiletries with mechanical precision. It's a habit by now, this packing-up-and-moving-on thing. I could probably do it blindfolded.

But as I zip the bag halfway closed, I freeze.

Liam's wish echoes in my mind.

To find a family to dream with.

My fingers grip the edge of the bag like it's the only thing keeping me grounded. The fabric digs into my palms, the strain spreading up my arms. If I can just hold on tight enough, maybe I can keep the emotions roiling in my chest from spilling out.

But they're there, pressing against me, impossible to ignore.

I don't want to think about him. About this place. About the way the last few weeks have crept into my heart and twisted something I thought was unshakable. For years, my answer to everything has been to leave—leave the place, leave the people, leave before I can get hurt or stuck or disappointed.

But here, in this quiet, messy, imperfect trailer park, I've started to see something I didn't think I wanted. A place where neighbors bicker like family. A girl who trusts me like I belong here. A man whose wish for something simple feels like a lifeline I didn't realize I needed.

I close my eyes, the edges of the bag blurring as tears threaten to spill.

For the first time in years, the questions I've been pushing away start clawing their way to the surface. Am I running toward something—or away from it?

And if I leave now, what am I really leaving behind?

The heater groans to life suddenly, breaking the silence with a rattling hum. I release the bag, my fingers aching from the tension, and sink onto the edge of the bed.

The words on that slip of paper loop endlessly in my mind, but they're joined by another thought, quieter but insistent.

Maybe I don't have to run this time.

Maybe… I could stay.

Have I been running toward something?

Or away from it?

The weight of the question makes my chest tighten. I stare at the bag, half-packed and waiting, but the answers don't come. The clothes inside seem to taunt me, little pieces of my life I've folded and unfolded so many times they've lost all meaning.

The heater rattles to life again, a dull hum filling the silence, but it doesn't chase away the cold sinking into my bones.

The faint creak of a floorboard behind me breaks through my thoughts.

"What's this?"

Liam's voice cuts through the quiet, low and sharp, startling me enough that I whirl around, my heart hammering against my ribs. He's standing in the doorway, his frame filling the space, his presence as steady as it is disarming. The cold air he brought in clings to him, a faint mist curling around his shoulders before dissipating.

His eyes aren't on me. They're locked on the bag sitting open on the bed, his expression shifting from confusion to something harder.

"Liam?" I blurt, my heart pounding. "What are you doing here?"

His gaze doesn't waver from the bag. "You're packing," he says flatly, ignoring the question.

I cross my arms, trying to mask my confusion—and the flicker of guilt twisting in my stomach. "Seriously, what are you doing here?"

For a second, I think he might answer, but instead, he steps further inside, his boots thudding softly against the floor. His focus narrows on the bag, the muscles in his jaw tightening with every step he takes.

"You're leaving."

"It's nothing," I say quickly, but the words sound hollow even to me.

His jaw sets, his tone sharper now. "Looks like something."

I force a laugh, hoping to brush it off, but it comes out too light, too brittle. "Relax, I'm just organizing."

"Organizing," he repeats, the disbelief clear in his voice. He steps closer, the tension in his body radiating across the small space between us. His gaze flicks from the bag to my face, and when his eyes meet mine, there's something there I can't quite name. Hurt? Anger?

"Ellie," he says, his voice low, but there's an edge to it that cuts deep. "You're leaving."

"I'm not," I insist, though my voice wavers. "Not yet."

"Not yet," he echoes, and this time, the bitterness in his tone is impossible to miss. "So you've got a timeline, then?"

His words hit harder than they should, and I hate that I can't find a way to argue. The truth is, I don't know what I'm doing. My mind is a mess of what-ifs and maybes, and none of it feels solid enough to hold onto.

"I..." The word hangs in the air, unfinished, useless.

Liam shakes his head, his eyes hardening. "You know what? Forget it."

He turns sharply, his shoulders rigid, and the sound of his boots against the floor is like thunder in the quiet.

"Liam, wait—"

But he's already gone, the door shutting behind him with a finality that leaves me breathless.

I stand frozen for a moment, the echo of his departure lingering in the stillness. The air in the trailer feels heavier now, like it's pressing down on me, making it impossible to move.

Finally, I sink onto the edge of the bed, staring at the half-packed bag as if it holds the answers I'm too scared to admit I need.

This is why I don't stay. Why I don't let myself get attached.

Because staying means risking everything.

I rub my hands over my face, the weight of the past weeks crashing down all at once. I think about Lila's laughter echoing through the hall, the way she handed me craft supplies like it was a piece of her heart. I think about Gloria, her relentless optimism in the face of losing everything she's worked so hard to protect.

And I think about Liam, standing in my doorway, his voice sharp and his eyes full of questions I didn't have the courage to answer.

Because the truth is, I don't want to leave.

Not really.

I look at the bag again, its zipper gaping like an accusation. For years, it's been my lifeline, always ready for the next escape. But now, for the first time, it feels like an anchor—like the weight of it might pull me under if I let it.

My gaze drifts to the window, where the lights from the park flicker faintly against the dark. Somewhere out there, the community is still buzzing with life, neighbors chatting over fences and kids daring each other to sprint across the snowy lawns.

I want to be a part of it.

The realization is small, quiet, but it roots itself deep in my chest.

Maybe I don't have to run this time.

Maybe... I could stay.

Chapter Eight

Holding Back

Liam Brookes

I shouldn't have gone to her trailer last night.

I should've stayed home, let the whole thing go, and reminded myself that Ellie Harper is not my problem.

But no, I had to head over there because Gloria mentioned Ellie seemed distracted, and for some reason, I thought that meant I should check on her. Like an idiot, I thought maybe she needed someone to talk to.

Instead, I walked in like some jealous fool, jumping to conclusions the second I saw that bag sitting open on her bed.

Now, I can't get the look on her face out of my head—the flash of guilt, the hesitation, the way her voice wavered when she said, *Not yet.*

Not yet.

It's as good as saying she's leaving. And why wouldn't she? She's been counting down the days since she got here, always talking about the city and her big plans.

I should've known better.

I spend most of the morning avoiding her.

It's easy enough. There's plenty to do—repairs to finish, decorations to double-check, tables to set up for the potluck. The hall's a hive of activity, neighbors bustling in and out with casseroles, desserts, and trays of drinks.

"Liam!" Gloria's voice cuts through the noise, sharp as ever. "I need you to fix the fairy lights by the stage. They're flickering again."

I nod and head toward the corner, grateful for the distraction. I grab the ladder and climb up, the steady rhythm of tightening bulbs giving my hands something to do, even if my mind refuses to settle.

But even as I work, my thoughts keep drifting back to Ellie.

I catch glimpses of her throughout the day—helping Doris arrange desserts, laughing with Ed over something I can't hear, sketching on the back of a paper plate. She looks... at home.

But I know better.

People like Ellie don't stay.

"Gloria, I don't know if I can do this."

Her voice cuts through my spiraling thoughts, freezing me mid-step.

I've just finished fixing the lights and am about to leave the hall when I catch sight of her and Gloria talking near the supply closet.

"You don't know if you can do what?" Gloria asks, hands on her hips, her tone sharper than usual.

"This," Ellie says, gesturing vaguely to the room around her. "The potluck, the park, all of it. I'm not... this isn't my kind of place."

Gloria raises an eyebrow, the lines of exhaustion etched deeper into her face than I've noticed before. "And what kind of place is your kind of place?"

Ellie falters, crossing her arms. "I don't know. The city, maybe? Somewhere bigger. Somewhere with more options."

Gloria lets out a sharp laugh, brittle and bitter. "Options, huh? You think we've got options here? Because from where I'm standing, the only option we've got is to fight like hell to keep our homes."

Ellie flinches at the edge in Gloria's voice, guilt flashing across her face.

"Look," Ellie says, shifting uncomfortably. "I didn't mean—"

"No, you didn't mean," Gloria interrupts, stepping closer. Her hands tighten into fists at her sides, her voice trembling now, the frustration bleeding into something raw. "You don't get it, do you? You have no idea what it's like to live with the thought that someone could come along and take everything away. This place isn't perfect, but it's *ours*. For some of us, it's all we've got."

Ellie's mouth opens, but no words come out. She looks away, her arms folding tighter across her chest like she's trying to hold herself together.

For a moment, Gloria's anger wavers, her posture softening just enough to reveal the exhaustion beneath it.

"You have people here," Gloria continues, her voice quieter now but no less fierce. "You have options. You can leave. But some of us? We don't get that luxury. So forgive me if I don't have patience for your city dreams right now, Ellie Harper."

The words land heavy in the quiet that follows.

Ellie takes a shaky breath, her gaze fixed on the floor. "I didn't mean to sound ungrateful," she says finally, her voice barely audible.

"Then maybe start acting like you care," Gloria snaps, but there's no venom in it this time. Just weariness.

The air between them feels thick enough to cut, and I should leave—should walk out and let them deal with this without me.

But I don't.

Instead, I clear my throat, stepping out from where I've been hovering near the stage. Both women look up, startled, and for a moment, no one speaks.

Ellie's face is pale, her hands gripping the edge of the table beside her like it's the only thing keeping her upright.

"Gloria," I say, keeping my voice calm, "why don't you take a break? Let me finish up here."

Gloria hesitates, her gaze flicking between Ellie and me before she lets out a sigh. "Fine. But don't think I'm done," she mutters, jabbing a finger in Ellie's direction before turning and marching toward the door.

Once she's gone, the silence stretches between us, heavier than before.

"I didn't mean for that to happen," Ellie says softly, her eyes darting to mine before quickly looking away. "I wasn't trying to—"

"I know," I interrupt, my tone firmer than I intend. "But she's not wrong."

Her head snaps up, her eyes narrowing. "Excuse me?"

"This isn't just some potluck, Ellie," I say, stepping closer. "It's more than decorations and casserole dishes. For a lot of people here, it's a way to fight for what matters. For what they can't afford to lose."

Her lips press into a thin line, and I can see the tension radiating through her shoulders. But instead of snapping back, she exhales slowly, her posture deflating.

"I don't know if I'm the right person for this," she admits, her voice barely above a whisper.

"Maybe you're not," I say, my words softening as I hold her gaze. "But you're here. And that counts for something."

She looks at me for a long moment, something flickering in her expression—uncertainty, maybe. Or resolve.

And then, without another word, she turns and walks toward the sketchpad she left on the table, picking up a pencil with hands that aren't quite steady.

I watch her for a moment before turning back to the lights.

Maybe Gloria's right.

Maybe this park doesn't have options.

But Ellie Harper? She does.

And I can't figure out whether I want her to take them—or stay right where she is.

* * *

I spend the rest of the afternoon outside, fixing the sign at the park's entrance. It's one of those simple jobs that doesn't take much thought, just steady hands and a rhythm to fall into. The creak of the ladder, the scrape of sandpaper on weathered wood, the occasional crunch of snow underfoot—it all keeps me grounded, keeps the storm in my head from taking over completely.

The sign itself isn't much to look at, just a wooden post with faded lettering that reads *Maple Creek Trailer Park.* Over the years, the paint has chipped, the edges have warped, and the entire thing leans slightly to the left. But it's ours.

As I repaint the letters, the brush gliding over the wood in smooth, deliberate strokes, I catch myself thinking about Ellie. About the way her voice wavered when Gloria laid into her earlier, the way she squared her shoulders like she was bracing for a fight she didn't know how to finish.

She's a contradiction. Tough and unsure, open one moment and closed off the next.

By the time I pack up and head back to the hall, the sun is slipping behind the horizon, painting the sky in streaks of lavender and gold. The air is colder now, sharp against my skin, but the bite of it is almost welcome. It keeps me awake, alert, focused on the here and now instead of the questions clawing at the edges of my mind.

The hall is buzzing when I step inside.

Laughter bounces off the walls, mingling with the clatter of dishes and the hum of conversation. The smell of roasted turkey and baked pies fills the air, warm and inviting, making it easy to forget the chill outside.

My boots echo against the floorboards as I make my way toward the back, scanning the room automatically.

And then I see her.

Ellie's near the stage, holding a box of sparklers, her hair tumbling over her shoulders in loose waves that catch the warm glow of the overhead lights. She's smiling—not the polite kind she wears when she's trying to keep her distance, but a real, unguarded smile that makes something catch in my chest.

She glances up and catches me watching.

For a moment, the noise of the room fades.

Her eyes meet mine, and something flickers between us. It's not loud or obvious, just a quiet shift in the air, like the first drop of rain before a storm.

I don't move, and neither does she.

The sparklers in her hands glint faintly in the light, the edges of the box catching like a promise half-formed. She tilts her head slightly, her lips curving into something softer, something almost shy.

And just like that, I feel it.

The pull.

It's the same one that's been there since the night her trailer broke down, the same one I've been trying to ignore ever since.

But here, now, with the way she's looking at me, it's harder to push it aside.

Someone calls her name, breaking the moment.

Ellie turns, her attention drawn to Gloria, who's waving her over with a clipboard in hand. She nods, laughing softly at something

Gloria says, and starts toward her, the box of sparklers tucked under her arm.

I exhale, the spell broken but the weight of it still lingering.

She doesn't look like someone planning to leave.

But then again, neither did she when she unpacked that sketchpad earlier, her pencil flying across the page like she belonged here. And yet, there was still that bag, half-packed and waiting.

I lean against the wall, crossing my arms as I watch her move through the room. She fits here in a way I can't explain—laughing with Doris over the dessert table, trading jokes with Ed as he adjusts the garlands above the windows.

And yet, there's a part of her that still feels untouchable. Like she's got one foot out the door, even when she's standing still.

Gloria waves her clipboard at me now, gesturing toward a table of mismatched decorations. I push off the wall and start toward her, but not before glancing back at Ellie.

She's by the kids' table now, crouching to help Lila untangle a string of lights.

Lila says something that makes her laugh again, and this time, she tilts her head back, her hair falling in a cascade over her shoulder.

It's a sound I want to hear again.

But I can't trust that feeling—not yet.

Not when the memory of that bag still lingers, a bruise that hasn't quite healed.

I turn away, reaching for the box Gloria thrusts into my hands, but even as I get back to work, my thoughts don't leave her.

* * *

Ellie stays late, helping Gloria and a few others finalize the setup. By the time the hall empties out, it's just the two of us, the hum of the heater filling the quiet space. The tables are set, the decorations sparkle under the dim overhead lights, and there's a faint scent of cinnamon lingering in the air.

It should feel like a job well done. Instead, it feels unfinished, like there's something left unsaid between us, hanging in the space where laughter and chatter had been just moments ago.

"I'm staying," she says suddenly, her voice cutting through the quiet like the strike of a match.

I glance up from the table I'm folding, her words catching me off guard. "What?"

"For the potluck and the fireworks," she clarifies, her tone steady but quieter than usual, like she's weighing each word carefully before letting it out. "I want to see it through."

I nod, unsure of what to say. The logical part of me knows this is good news—great news, even. But my chest tightens anyway, the relief tainted by something heavier.

"After that..." She trails off, her gaze dropping to the sparklers lying on the table between us. Her fingers brush over one absentmindedly, tracing its edges like she's trying to ground herself. "I don't know. But for now, I'm staying."

Her words settle over me, each one a tiny ripple in the air. They should make me feel better, but they don't.

Because *for now* isn't forever. And I don't know if I'm ready to watch her leave again.

I press my palm flat against the table, the edge of the wood digging into my hand. "That's... good," I say finally, the words coming out slower than I mean them to.

Ellie looks up at me then, her eyes catching the soft glow of the lights overhead. There's something in her expression I can't quite name—hope, maybe, or uncertainty. Or maybe it's the same tangled mess of emotions that's been clawing at me since the night I saw her packing that bag.

I drop my gaze to the sparklers, focusing on the delicate sticks of wire and glitter instead of the way she's looking at me.

She's not going to stay. Not really. She's already told me as much.

And yet...

The thought of her leaving twists something inside me, sharp and insistent, refusing to be ignored. I can picture it too clearly—her trailer pulling away, her laughter fading into memory, this tiny spark of warmth she's brought into the park going with her.

I don't want her to go.

The realization hits me hard, slamming into my chest like a physical weight.

I don't just want Ellie Harper to stay.

I need her to stay.

She's burrowed her way into my life, into Lila's life, into this little corner of the world I've always tried so hard to protect. And now, the idea of her being anywhere else feels... wrong.

The thought is terrifying.

And yet, it's also steadying in a way I don't understand.

I love her.

The words settle in my chest, unspoken but undeniable. They fit, even though I don't know what to do with them yet.

"I'm glad you're staying," I say, my voice low but steady. "For the potluck. And the fireworks."

Her lips curve into a small smile, and for a second, I let myself believe it's because of me. Not the fireworks, not the potluck, just... me.

"Me too," she murmurs, her fingers still idly playing with the sparklers.

The room feels smaller now, the space between us charged with something I can't name but don't want to lose.

"I should probably head out," she says, breaking the spell.

I nod, stepping aside to let her pass. But as she moves toward the door, I catch myself speaking without thinking. "Ellie."

She pauses, turning back to face me.

I hesitate, the words catching in my throat. What am I supposed to say? That I don't want her to leave? That I'm half in love with her already, even though I've spent most of my time trying to keep my distance?

"Be careful," I say finally, the words falling short of everything I want to tell her.

She tilts her head, studying me for a moment before nodding. "I will."

And then she's gone, the door clicking shut behind her, leaving me alone in the hall with nothing but the hum of the heater and the ache in my chest.

I stare at the sparklers on the table, their silver coating glinting faintly under the lights. They're small, delicate, fleeting.

Just like Ellie, I think bitterly.

But then I remember the way she smiled when she said she was staying. The way her voice softened, like maybe, just maybe, she wanted to believe it too.

I pick up one of the sparklers, rolling it between my fingers. It feels too light, too fragile to hold the weight of everything I want to say.

Chapter Nine

Fireworks and Forever

Ellie Harper

The community hall glows like something out of a storybook. Strings of twinkling lights drape the rafters, casting a warm, golden glow over the room. The tables are dressed with centerpieces I designed—tiny snow globes with miniature trailers inside, each one unique. The lights catch on the glitter in the globes, sending faint sparkles dancing across the ceiling like tiny stars.

I step back, surveying the room as neighbors laugh and chat, their voices blending with the soft hum of holiday music. The air smells like cinnamon and fresh pine, the faintest hint of Ed's famous casserole wafting in from the buffet table.

It's... perfect.

Not perfect like the city parties I used to imagine myself planning, with their champagne fountains and high-end glamour. But perfect in a way that feels real, like the kind of memory you hold onto years later and smile about.

Gloria bustles up to me, beaming, her cheeks flushed from a mix of excitement and the warmth of the crowded hall. "Ellie, this is beautiful. You've outdone yourself."

"Thanks," I say, trying not to blush under her praise.

"No, I mean it," she insists, gripping my arm like she needs me to feel the weight of her words. "You've given this place life. Look at everyone—they're smiling because of you."

I glance around the room again, my gaze catching on little moments: Lila showing off a sparkler to a group of kids, Ed and Doris sharing a rare, unguarded laugh as they sway to the music near the corner, Gloria practically glowing as she leaves my side to chat animatedly with Councilman Greene.

The atmosphere feels lighter than it has in weeks, like the whole park has exhaled a breath it didn't know it was holding.

For the first time in a long time, I feel like I've done something that matters.

When the potluck winds down, the crowd spills outside, bundled in coats and scarves as we gather in the clearing for the fireworks. The cold bites at my cheeks, but the warmth of the night lingers in my chest, chasing away the chill.

Lila stands beside me, bouncing on her toes with excitement, her face glowing under the faint light of the moon. "Ellie, this is my favorite part! You're going to love it."

"I can't wait," I tell her, my smile widening as she grabs my hand, her enthusiasm contagious.

Liam lingers a few feet away, his breath curling into the cold air. His expression is unreadable—steady, as always—but there's something about the way he stands, his hands stuffed deep into his pockets, that feels... careful. Like he's trying to keep just enough space between us to remind me where we stand.

When he catches me looking at him, though, something in his gaze softens. He steps closer, the space between us narrowing until the cold air feels less like a barrier and more like a fragile boundary waiting to be crossed.

A burst of laughter from the crowd draws my attention to the side, where Councilman Greene stands in the midst of a group of neighbors. He's holding a plate of food—likely Ed's famous casserole, judging by the way Ed is hovering nearby—and nodding enthusiastically as Gloria regales him with one of her many stories.

He's smiling.

Not just a polite, political smile, but a real one, the kind that reaches his eyes and makes him look like he's genuinely enjoying himself.

"Looks like he's having a good time," I murmur, leaning slightly toward Liam without even thinking about it.

Liam follows my gaze, his lips twitching in what might be a smile—or a smirk. "Gloria probably wore him down."

I laugh softly, but it's true. Gloria has been relentless all night, introducing him to every family, sharing stories about the history of the park, and even getting him to add his wish to the fireworks jar.

Across the clearing, Greene gestures toward the hall, his voice carrying just enough for me to catch a snippet: "This is exactly the kind of community we need more of."

My breath catches, and I glance at Liam, who's clearly heard it too.

"Do you think..." I start, but I don't finish the question.

Liam shrugs, his expression softer now, almost hopeful. "If anyone can win him over, it's Gloria. And, well, all of this." He gestures to the scene around us—the glowing lights, the laughter, the neighbors mingling like a family.

As the countdown begins, the crowd gathers tightly, their voices weaving into an electric hum. I glance over and see Greene standing apart now, his head tilted back as he watches the sky.

It's quiet awe, the kind that isn't put on for anyone's benefit. In that moment, I know he feels it too—the magic of this place.

"Let's just say," Liam murmurs, leaning closer, his voice low and warm, "I wouldn't want to be the developer trying to convince him otherwise after tonight."

I smile, the tension in my chest easing for the first time in what feels like weeks.

And in that moment, I know.

The park is going to be okay.

The crowd's voices surge together as if the countdown itself could push away the weight of the past year.

"Ten!"

Liam stands just a few feet away, his broad shoulders rising and falling in rhythm with his steady breaths. Clouds of vapor curl into the cold night air, lit faintly by the glow of the nearby sparklers. His jaw is tight, his posture careful, like he's holding back an entire avalanche of words.

But his eyes—they're on me.

"Nine!"

"I need to say something," he says suddenly, his voice low but sharp enough to slice through the growing noise.

I blink, startled by the urgency in his tone. He takes a step closer, the snow crunching softly under his boots, and it feels like the distance between us isn't just physical.

"Eight!"

All around us, conversations fade. It's subtle at first, a few glances here and there, but soon even Lila stops mid-bounce, her sparkler frozen in her hand. She looks up at us with wide, curious eyes, her excitement giving way to quiet anticipation.

"Ellie," Liam begins, his voice steady despite the way his hands fidget in his coat pockets. "When you first came here, I thought you were just passing through. Another person with big dreams and no reason to stay."

"Seven!"

His words hit me like a wave, pulling at every defense I've built since the day I arrived. My chest tightens, and I can't seem to force a single word past the lump forming in my throat.

"Six!"

"I thought I was fine with that," Liam continues, his gaze unwavering as it locks onto mine. "Because people leave. That's just what they do."

"Five!"

There's a faint tremor in his voice, and I realize he's holding his breath, like he's afraid the next word might undo him. But then he straightens, his shoulders squaring as he pushes forward.

"But then you showed up," he says, his tone softening as he gestures faintly toward the hall behind us, "with your glitter and your snow globes and your big ideas. And suddenly, this place didn't feel the same. It felt... brighter."

"Four!"

The noise of the crowd seems to dull as the weight of his words settles over me. His expression is open, raw in a way I've never seen before, and it makes my heart ache in a way that's both terrifying and exhilarating.

"Three!"

"Fireworks are fleeting," Liam says, his voice dropping lower, fuller, wrapping around me like a blanket. "They burn bright for a moment, and then they're gone. But you... you make me believe in something lasting."

"Two!"

The crowd's cheers grow louder, but they're a distant hum against the pounding of my heart. My world has narrowed to him—his words, his gaze, the quiet determination that threads through every syllable.

"One!"

"Ellie," he says, his voice breaking slightly, raw with emotion. "I don't want you to leave. I want you to stay. With me."

The crowd erupts in cheers as the clock strikes midnight, a burst of noise and celebration that makes the earth itself feel alive.

Fireworks streak across the sky in a cascade of light and color, their explosions painting the snow with shimmering hues. Around us, neighbors hug and laugh, their voices blending with the crackle of sparklers and the low rumble of the fireworks.

But I can't move.

Can't think.

His words—*Stay. With me.*—echo in my mind, louder than the fireworks, louder than the cheers.

I glance at Lila, who's waving her sparkler again, her laughter bright and unrestrained. Around us, the glow of the community hall casts a warm light on familiar faces, each one filled with joy and hope for the year ahead.

And then I look back at Liam.

His hand is outstretched, tentative, like he's not sure I'll take it. His expression is open, vulnerable, and it's like every grumpy wall he's ever built has been stripped away, leaving only the man I've been seeing glimpses of all along.

The man I've been falling for, whether I wanted to admit it or not.

I take a breath, the cold air sharp and grounding, and I step closer.

"You're wrong," I say softly, my voice just loud enough for him to hear.

His brow furrows, confusion flickering across his face.

"You're wrong about fireworks," I continue, lifting my hand to brush against his. "They don't just burn bright and disappear. They leave a mark. They stay with you."

His eyes widen, his breath catching as my fingers curl around his.

"And so do you," I whisper.

The noise around us fades into the background as he pulls me closer, his arms wrapping around me like they've been waiting for this moment as long as I have.

His lips find mine, soft and sure, and for the first time, I feel like I've found my place.

The fireworks above burst into a finale, the sky shimmering with a thousand colors.

Chapter Ten

A Morning to Begin

Liam Brookes

The morning light filters through the kitchen window, soft and golden, spilling across the worn wooden table like a quiet promise. It catches the edges of the coffee mugs, turning the rising steam into faint, curling trails that drift upward before vanishing. The frost on the window glints faintly, stubborn and reluctant to yield, but the sun's persistence is already working to chase it away.

Ellie sits across from me, her hands wrapped around her mug like it's a lifeline, her fingers nearly swallowed by the oversized sleeves of her sweater. Her hair is a chaotic mess from sleep, strands curling every which way in a way that somehow suits her perfectly. She doesn't try to fix it in the mornings, and I hope she never does.

The room is quiet, save for the faint tick of the clock on the wall and the occasional creak of the heater kicking on. But it's the kind of quiet that doesn't ask for anything. It just exists, like a steady rhythm that lets you breathe without thinking about it.

For the first time in years, I feel... steady.

Ellie shifts in her seat, her sleepy smile breaking the stillness. "I can't believe it's January first already."

I chuckle, leaning back in my chair and stretching my legs under the table. "Feels like we packed a year into the last week."

She laughs softly, a warm, unhurried sound that spreads through the room like sunlight after a long storm. Her laugh has a way of settling into the quiet, making it fuller somehow, like it belongs there.

"Yeah," she says, her voice thoughtful now. "A lot happened."

Her gaze drifts toward the window, where the frost clings stubbornly to the glass but is beginning to give way under the sun's gentle persistence. She traces her finger along the rim of her mug, her brow furrowing slightly, as though she's working through a thought she hasn't quite put into words yet.

"It's weird," she murmurs, breaking the silence again. "I always thought the city was where I'd find everything I wanted. But now... I don't know. This place feels different. Like maybe it could be enough."

"It's more than enough," I say, my voice quiet but firm.

Her head turns, and our eyes meet across the table. For a moment, I see something in her expression—something raw, open, searching. It's like she's finally letting herself see what I've known all along. This isn't just a place. It's a home.

Before either of us can say anything more, there's a sudden crash from the next room, followed by Lila's unmistakable giggle.

"Lila!" I call, setting my mug down as the sound of hurried footsteps echoes closer. "What are you doing?"

"Nothing!" comes her singsong reply, which I've learned is her code for *absolutely something*.

Ellie raises an eyebrow, a grin tugging at her lips. "Should we be worried?"

"Always," I mutter, pushing back my chair just as Lila bursts into the kitchen.

Her curls bounce wildly as she skids to a stop, her cheeks flushed with excitement. She's wearing one of those sparkly sweaters Gloria probably bought her—this one in a festive silver that makes her look like a walking New Year's Eve decoration. In her hands, she's clutching what looks like an impossibly long sheet of paper, painted with bold, bright colors and doused liberally in glitter.

"Ta-da!" she announces, unfurling it with a dramatic flourish.

The banner stretches across the room, the words *Fireworks and Forever* scrawled in wobbly, glittery letters. Hand-drawn fireworks burst in the corners, their vibrant reds and golds catching the morning light and sending tiny flecks of sparkle scattering over the floor.

Ellie gasps softly, her hand flying to her mouth. "Lila, did you make this?"

"Yep!" Lila beams, holding it up proudly. "I thought we could hang it in the community hall. Or... maybe here, if you're staying."

Ellie's eyes flick to mine, her expression softening into something unspoken but hopeful.

"I love it," she says, standing to take the banner from Lila's hands. "It's perfect."

Lila basks in the praise for all of two seconds before skipping off, no doubt in search of more glitter or another masterpiece to create.

Ellie watches her go, shaking her head with a smile that lingers even as she turns back to me. She brushes her fingers lightly over the banner, tracing the glittery letters. "She's something else."

"She gets it from her mom," I say, my voice soft. Then, after a pause, I add, "And maybe a little from you, too."

Ellie's cheeks flush pink, and she ducks her head, pretending to study the banner more closely. But I see the way her lips curve, unable to hide her smile.

I step closer, reaching out to gently take her hand, my thumb brushing over hers. "What do you think?" I ask, nodding toward the banner. "Does it feel like it could fit here?"

She tilts her head, her gaze lifting to meet mine. "Here?"

"Yeah," I say, my voice quieter now. "With us."

Her smile falters, just for a second, and I can see the hesitation in her eyes—the fear of hoping for something she's not sure she can hold onto.

"You think it'll work?" she asks, barely above a whisper.

"Ellie," I say, brushing a strand of hair from her face, "it's already working."

Her smile returns, tentative but real, and she leans into me, letting me pull her closer.

"I love it," she says, standing to take the banner from Lila's hands. "It's perfect."

Lila basks in the praise for all of two seconds before skipping off, her curls bouncing as she hums a tune that sounds vaguely like "Auld Lang Syne." She disappears down the hallway, probably on the hunt for more glitter or another project to turn the kitchen table into a disaster zone.

Ellie watches her go, shaking her head with a smile that lingers even as she turns back to me. She brushes her fingers lightly over the banner, tracing the glittery letters as if committing each one to memory. "She's something else."

"She gets it from her mom," I say, my voice softer than I intended. Then, after a pause, I add, "And maybe a little from you, too."

Ellie's cheeks flush pink, and she ducks her head, pretending to study the banner more closely. But I see the way her lips curve, the way she bites back a smile like she's not quite ready to let it show completely.

I step closer, the quiet of the room amplifying the sound of my footsteps on the worn wooden floor. My fingers brush hers as I take her hand, my thumb gliding over the ridge of her knuckles. "What do you think?" I ask, nodding toward the banner still draped in her arms. "Does it feel like it could fit here?"

She tilts her head, her gaze lifting to meet mine. "Here?"

"Yeah," I say, my voice quieter now. "With us."

Her smile falters, just for a second, and I can see the hesitation in her eyes—the fear of hoping for something she's not sure she can hold onto. It's a look I know too well because I've worn it myself more times than I can count.

"You think it'll work?" she asks, her voice barely above a whisper, like saying the words too loud might break the fragile possibility hanging between us.

"Ellie," I say, brushing a strand of hair from her face, "it's already working."

Her smile returns, tentative but real, and she leans into me, her weight soft and certain as I pull her closer.

Later, we stand together by the window, the banner carefully draped over the back of the couch like it's waiting for its official debut. Outside, the frost continues to melt, revealing tiny glimpses of green beneath the thinning snow. The sunlight catches on the icicles still clinging stubbornly to the eaves, turning them into shards of crystal that glimmer faintly against the brightening sky.

"This feels right," Ellie murmurs, her head resting against my shoulder.

I press a kiss to her temple, letting my arm tighten around her waist. "It does."

She tilts her head to look up at me, her eyes searching mine, and for a moment, the world narrows to just this—her gaze, her warmth, the quiet promise threaded between us.

"Do you think we can make it work? Really work?"

My smile widens as I brush my thumb along her cheek, the faint warmth of her skin grounding me. "We've got fireworks, Ellie. The kind that last."

Her laugh is quiet, but it lights something deep in my chest, steady and bright, the kind of feeling that lingers long after the moment has passed.

The sun climbs higher, chasing away the last of the frost, and as the light streams in, Ellie turns to me with a certainty that makes me want to stop time just to hold this moment longer.

"It's funny," she says, her voice thoughtful. "I used to think I'd always be chasing something. That I'd never feel settled. But here, with you and Lila… it doesn't feel like settling. It feels like building."

"You're not chasing anymore," I reply. "You're home."

Her smile deepens, and she leans up on her toes to press a kiss to my jaw, her breath warm against my skin.

From somewhere in the distance, Gloria's voice echoes faintly, calling out instructions to no one in particular. It's probably about the decorations for the community hall or a last-minute scheme to make the New Year's potluck even more extravagant than it already is.

Ellie laughs softly, shaking her head. "Do you think she'll ever slow down?"

"Not a chance," I say with a grin. "But we wouldn't want her to."

She tilts her head, her gaze turning serious for a moment. "Do you think we're ready for all of this? For forever?"

I take her hand, lacing our fingers together as I hold her gaze. "Forever doesn't have to happen all at once. We'll take it one day at a time. Together."

Her laughter is light, but it carries a weight that feels like a promise.

"Happy New Year, Liam," she says softly.

"Happy New Year, Ellie," I reply, leaning down to kiss her.

The kiss is slow, unhurried, like we've got all the time in the world. And maybe we do. Because this isn't just the start of a new year.

It's the start of forever.

Chapter Eleven

Epilogue

The sky above Maple Creek glitters with fireworks, brilliant bursts of red, gold, and silver reflecting off the fresh snow blanketing the ground. The air hums with excitement, every distant pop and crackle a celebration of the year that's ending and the one about to begin.

Ellie Brookes—formerly Ellie Harper—stands at the edge of the clearing, bundled in a long coat, a scarf wrapped snugly around her neck. Wisps of her breath curl into the crisp winter air, her cheeks flushed from the cold. She tilts her head back, watching a golden burst fade into a thousand tiny sparks, her lips curling into a contented smile.

It's hard to believe it's been five years since she first stumbled into this park. So much has changed—yet so much has stayed the same.

Behind her, the community hall hums with life, its windows glowing with warm light. Laughter and music spill into the night, mingling with the distant echoes of fireworks. The annual New Year's potluck is in full swing, a tradition Ellie has grown to cherish.

Inside, she knows Gloria is holding court near the dessert table, likely bossing someone into submission over pie placement. Ed and Doris are probably arguing about something trivial—another casserole-related debate, no doubt—while Lila darts from group to group, her boundless energy lighting up every corner.

Ellie stepped outside for a moment of quiet, needing to take it all in. To let the weight of the moment settle over her.

This little park, with its mismatched trailers and quirky traditions, has become everything she once thought she didn't need: a home.

"Mom!"

Lila's voice cuts through the stillness, high and cheerful, pulling Ellie from her thoughts.

She turns just as Lila runs up to her, her breath puffing in the cold as she waves something through the air. At thirteen, Lila is taller now, her frame more willowy, but the sparkle in her eyes and her mischievous grin haven't changed a bit.

"Look!" Lila exclaims, holding up a small sparkler. Its golden light flickers brightly, tiny sparks hissing as they fall away.

Ellie laughs softly. "Aren't you supposed to save those for the countdown?"

"Dad said I could use one now," Lila replies, her smile widening. "He said it's a 'test run.'"

Ellie shakes her head fondly. "Sounds like him."

"Speaking of," Lila says, grabbing Ellie's hand and tugging her toward the hall. "Dad says you're going to miss the best part if you stay out here!"

"I'm coming," Ellie says with a laugh, letting herself be pulled along. "Is everyone ready?"

"Almost!" Lila chirps, her sparkler still hissing in her other hand. "Gloria says we're going to start the countdown soon, and I told her you can't miss it!"

The warmth from the hall hits Ellie as they step inside, the sounds of laughter and conversation wrapping around her like a well-worn blanket. She looks around, taking in the familiar faces and festive decorations, her heart swelling with a quiet kind of joy.

For years, she'd run from places like this. From anything that felt too permanent, too rooted.

But now, she couldn't imagine being anywhere else.

The hall hasn't changed much over the years, though Ellie's touch is evident in the elegant but cozy decorations. The tables are adorned with glittering centerpieces—a nod to her old sketches from years ago, ideas that once felt like little more than daydreams. Now, they shimmer under the soft glow of the overhead lights, catching the eyes of every passerby.

Banners proclaiming *"Fireworks and Forever"* hang proudly on the walls, their letters bold and glittering, a reflection of Ellie's vision and persistence.

Because Fireworks and Forever isn't just an idea anymore.

It's her business now.

The name she once scribbled in notebooks as a teenager, dreaming of a future that felt impossibly far away, is now printed on cards, posters, and even a bright sign outside her small office just outside the park. What began as a modest effort—planning weddings and birthday parties for friends and neighbors—has grown into something she could have never imagined.

Now, clients call from neighboring towns, asking for her magic touch to transform their events into something unforgettable. She's even had inquiries from businesses looking for that special spark only Ellie seems to create.

And the best part? She's doing it all here.

Not in some sprawling city or some place far from her roots. Here, at Maple Creek, with Liam and Lila by her side.

A warmth blooms in her chest as she takes in the scene around her—the chatter of neighbors, the laughter of children, the faint strains of music from the old speakers in the corner.

This place is everything she used to run from.

Now, it's everything she runs toward.

"Hey," Liam's voice draws her attention, soft and familiar, grounding her in the present.

She turns to see him walking toward her, his sleeves rolled up from whatever task Gloria had wrangled him into. His dark hair is slightly mussed, and there's a smudge of glitter on his forearm, a testament to the night's chaos. But his smile? It's the same as ever—steady and warm, as if nothing in the world could shake it.

"You okay?" he asks, slipping an arm around her waist and pulling her closer.

Ellie leans into him, letting his presence chase away the last remnants of her nerves. "I am now."

His brow quirks, his smile turning teasing. "Now? Was something wrong before?"

She laughs softly, resting her head on his shoulder for a moment. "Just taking it all in. It's a lot, you know?"

Liam glances around the room, his gaze lingering on the banners, the decorations, and finally, the people. "Yeah. But it's a good lot."

"A great lot," Ellie agrees, her smile widening as Lila races past them, her laugh ringing out above the crowd.

Liam presses a kiss to Ellie's temple, his voice low and filled with affection. "That's because you made it that way."

And as Ellie looks around the hall again, she knows he's right.

She made this life—one filled with fireworks, forever, and everything in between.

Lila bounces back over, her curls flying as she grabs both their hands, tugging them toward the front of the hall with boundless energy. "Come on! It's almost midnight!"

Ellie lets out a laugh, exchanging a look with Liam, whose mock-exasperated expression doesn't hide the fondness in his eyes. He shakes his head but follows Lila's lead, their joined hands swinging slightly as they make their way through the bustling crowd.

The hall is alive with chatter and laughter, neighbors pressing in close as everyone gathers near the makeshift stage. The warm light from the strings of twinkling bulbs overhead casts a golden glow on the crowd, making the moment feel almost dreamlike.

"Find a good spot!" Lila commands, pulling them to the center of the room before darting off to join the group of kids clustered near the stage. Her laughter rings out, bright and clear, as she waves her sparkler triumphantly.

Ellie watches her go, her heart swelling with something she can't quite put into words. The years have passed so quickly, each one filled with milestones and memories, but seeing Lila now—so full of joy and confidence—makes it all feel worth it.

Liam nudges her gently, his hand still in hers. "She's growing up too fast," he murmurs, his voice soft and edged with wistfulness.

Ellie nods, her throat tightening as she looks up at him. "Too fast," she agrees.

But before the weight of the thought can settle too deeply, someone shouts, "It's time!"

A hush falls over the crowd, replaced by a charged anticipation. The old speakers crackle slightly as Gloria's voice rings out, leading the countdown with theatrical flair.

"Ten!"

Ellie looks up at Liam, her heart full to the brim. The warmth of his hand in hers, the familiar steadiness of his presence—it's everything she never knew she needed.

"Nine!"

Lila squeezes their hands as she bounces back to them, her excitement so contagious Ellie can't help but smile.

"Eight!"

The years have passed so quickly, but Ellie wouldn't trade a single moment. Each one, even the hard ones, has brought her here, to this.

"Seven!"

Liam glances down at her, his eyes soft, the corners crinkling in that familiar way that always manages to melt her resolve. "Happy New Year, Ellie," he says, his voice low enough that only she can hear.

"Six!"

Her grin comes easily, warmth spreading from her chest outward, chasing away the chill of the winter night. "Happy New Year, Liam," she replies, her voice steady but filled with affection.

"Five!"

Outside, the first pops of fireworks break through the night air, vibrant bursts of red and gold painting the sky. The colors reflect off the snow, casting dancing patterns of light across the clearing and spilling faintly into the hall. The crowd murmurs in awe, the festive energy bubbling over.

"Four!"

Lila's voice cuts through the noise, high and insistent. "Wait! I need another sparkler!" She shouts something about finding the stash Gloria hid by the dessert table before darting off into the crowd, her laughter trailing behind her like a spark of its own.

Ellie watches her go, unable to help the smile that tugs at her lips. Lila is all energy and excitement, a whirlwind of light and joy.

"Three!"

Liam's arm tightens around Ellie's waist, his touch grounding her as the noise of the crowd fades into the background. He turns her slightly, facing her fully, and the world seems to shrink until it's just the two of them in their own private moment.

He leans down, his forehead resting gently against hers, their breaths mingling in the cold night air.

"Two!"

"I love you," he whispers, the words steady and unhurried, weaving through the noise around them like a familiar melody meant only for her.

Even after all these years, those words have the power to undo her. Her heart flutters, her pulse quickening as she leans into him, her guard slipping away entirely.

"One!"

www.ingramcontent.com/pod-product-compliance
Lightning Source LLC
LaVergne TN
LVHW010115170826
845678LV00012B/2413

* 9 7 9 8 2 3 0 2 6 6 3 0 3 *